AN ALIEN SPARK

CALLA ZAE

PROSE & CONCEPTS

AN ALIEN SPARK

SOLDIERS OF SAEDO 6

USA TODAY BESTSELLING AUTHOR

CALLA ZAE

An Alien Spark

Copyright © 2022 by Calla Zae

Cover Art Copyright: Calla Zae

Space Map Art Copyright: Calla Zae

Prose & Concepts LLC

210 Park Avenue, Suite #280

Worcester, MA 01609

www.proseandconcepts.com

This book is a work of fiction. All characters, places, names, and events are a product of the author's imagination. Any resemblance to events, locations, or persons alive or otherwise, is entirely coincidental.

Library of Congress Cataloging-in-Publication Data

Library of Congress Control Number: 2022935267

First edition Ebook ISBN: 978-1-952820-27-4

First edition Paperback ISBN: 978-1-952820-28-1

Audiobook ISBN: 978-1-952820-29-8

For those searching for their spark in life and love.

.

.

.

"The universe continually sends us sensory messages, which we can never quite decode."
— Susan Hubbard

ALARUS GALAXY MAP
PLANET CELERON

ONE

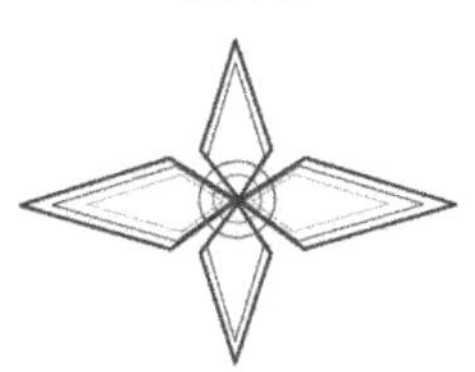

Feeling restless after a week of grueling work, Nina was ready for a break. Today was her first day off—well, sort of. She had just finished editing five new yoga videos and a small course for aliens that she'd uploaded onto the Galacto Net, a massive internet for the Cosmos.

It was still a bit weird for her to think of the internet connecting different galaxies where star-beings were watching her videos, even making some go viral. It was even weirder that these star-beings were commenting and requesting more videos from her, but she'd take whatever she could to establish herself on this new planet, Celeron.

Her sense of adventure had also returned. That was a good and bad thing. Its return meant that she was healing, and at the same time a reminder of how she had been wounded. As a yoga instructor, she tried to imagine her current situation as a difficult pose that took time, strength, and patience to master. Though her healing process was moving at a snail's pace, she was at least moving and not stagnating like she had back on Earth.

Living in Saedo gave her a new opportunity to remake herself. Nina Nelson deserved a second chance like everyone else.

She ignored the exhaustion in her limbs and headed to the huge marketplace down at the Village Center. She shrugged off the unease that made her wish she had stayed home to sleep. But today was the last day of the marketplace. Her artist sister, Rita, had told her about the octopus-being, Mikasso, offering free mini-sessions. She didn't want to miss this chance to see him demonstrate his sculpting skills. This was her first attempt at doing something fun, something adventurous—her artistic skills could pass for someone in kindergarten. Not that there was anything wrong with that.

Again, she was on a journey of healing. If that meant making ugly sculptures, so be it.

She strode into the marketplace, which was hosted inside a massive warehouse for vendors from all over Celeron. The active energy slammed into her, giving her the boost she needed. But she kept her eyes open for a coffee vendor to ensure she lasted the entire day.

Nina walked by booths that sold unique gifts from artists, sculptors, bakers, candle makers, blacksmiths, and fashion designers in Saedo. She saw the area reserved for StoryArt Gallery, but it was too crowded. She'd stop by later to check out Rita's paintings. Nina maneuvered around a group of tourists consisting of humanoids, cyborgs, and some reptilian beings with spiky tails to get a better view of Mikasso, who was demonstrating his new sculpture using some kind of innovative stone material.

Six months ago, she would never have thought she'd be standing among these spectacular beings on a planet NASA hadn't discovered yet. Never in her wildest dreams did she think aliens were real. But these star-beings had opened her mind. They had accepted her and her sisters onto their land, given them a place to live and jobs to support themselves. Most importantly, she and her six sisters each got a chance to start a new life, something they all desperately needed.

She could understand the universal language from the language translator inserted into her ear. She could read the universal language after a doctor had sent a beam of energy into her brain and activated the language codex. She didn't even know her brain was capable of something like that.

"The human brain is a marvel with infinite possibilities that hasn't been discovered yet," she recalled the doctor telling her when she was easily able to read an alien book. If only her other issues could be resolved with a beam of energy.

The crowd clapped when Mikasso used three of his tentacles to form an extraordinary sculpture that mimicked the two-headed volunteer boy standing beside him.

A slew of questions flew out from the audience.

"How much is the Stellar Saxum stone?"

"Is there a discount if we sign up for your virtual class today?"

"What's your refund policy?"

"You can speak to my rep over there. She'll have all the answers." Mikasso pointed to a dark green-skinned female star-being, who waved enthusiastically at everyone.

"You have ten tentacles—not including the feet you're standing on—that help you mold and create. I only have two arms and two legs. How can I achieve that level of detail like you, sir?" asked a female star-being with very skinny legs who stood beside a scaly-faced reptilian male.

"Practice, my dear." Mikasso held out a carving tool with one tentacle, while another sanded it with a glowing hand-held device. "Practice, practice, practice. That's what I had to do too. I've been sculpting for over fifty solar cycles. You'll get there too. Just give it time."

When he was done, silence filled the room as everyone gaped at the stunning sculpture.

"It looks just like you, Joojoo." The boy's mom tapped him on the head.

"It's for you." Mikasso curled the top layer of his lips into a smile. "Take it home. Thank you for volunteering. I know it takes courage to stand there with all eyes on you."

The boy offered a sheepish grin. "Thanks." He looked up at his mom. "Can I take his sculpting class, please? Can I? Please, please!"

Mikasso crouched. "You know what? Because you've demonstrated extraordinary courage and patience, I'll let you sign up for free. I'd love to have a student like you. You can sign up with my rep."

The boy threw his arms around Mikasso's legs. "Thank you very much, sir!"

Mikasso faced the audience. "We have a free lesson for the next hour in the conference room. You can make your own sculpture and take it home. Join if you'd like."

Nina didn't have to think twice. She followed the crowd into the conference room and found an empty chair at a table. A white stone about twelve inches high and eight inches wide sat on the table. Next to her were two young star-beings with orange hair watching a step-by-step video on how to carve. Their stones were brown and mossy green.

If these kids could do this, Nina could too.

Excitement thrilled her. She'd never sculpted anything. Well, kneading bread dough was sort of "sculpting" wasn't it?

Her sense of exploration had died not too long ago because of an ex-lover's opinion. Roger never wanted her to explore or do anything that made her happy. He had been overly competitive with her. Competition wasn't a bad thing; it pushed them to improve themselves. But he continually wanted her to do poorly just to make him look better, it became a major issue.

By the time Nina kicked Roger to the curb, the effect of what he did to her had already wrecked her self-esteem. She was still on the mend from that damage. She couldn't believe she had allowed him to stop her from taking classes that interested her—floral arrangements, interior design, landscaping, terrarium making, or even getting her yoga certificate. He wanted her to remain *useless*, someone who *needed* him. What kind of shitty man was that?

She never wanted to be with someone like him ever again. What kind of mental state had she been in to not see that glaring problem? Love was blind, indeed.

Roger didn't know that despite him discouraging her from learning yoga, she got her certificate without his knowledge. But she shouldn't have had to hide doing what she loved. She had a rebellious side that he obviously missed. That certification was the key to her freedom. She didn't need anyone's approval to do what her heart desired. She was a fantastic yoga instructor. And now, she was using that skill on a new planet. She wanted to try everything that appealed to her.

In Saedo, a lot of things appealed to her. Particularly one gorgeous soldier who had saved her and her sisters on that fateful New Year's Eve from the horrific Ulkrin aliens, whom she never wanted to encounter again.

Thinking about Zeycott gave her a boost of energy. From what she observed when he had been at her sister Sasha's house, he had a fantastic body. He had been helping Maeson, Sasha's lover, build a deck at the back of their new home. Zeycott's green skin fascinated her, especially his chest, shoulders, and arms, where he was covered in abstract tattoos.

She had never been attracted to men with tattoos until now. That was a "dangerous" façade that had kept her away. Was he a bad boy? Was he part of a gang? These were practical thoughts that had popped into her mind. She knew she shouldn't judge people like that, but society had conditioned her to think a certain way. Living here in Saedo, she'd tried to shed those notions. She was living among creatures with scales, spikes, and other textured patterns on their bodies, and these citizens all welcomed her and her sisters into their province.

She recalled one time she went to a friend's bachelorette party and came home with airbrushed tattoos on her arm. Roger had overreacted, saying she looked like a slut for desecrating her skin. After the floral design came off in three days, she never considered having art on her body again. But now, she was ready to reclaim herself. She wanted to step across that "danger zone," to know what was beyond it. It didn't matter what the consequences would be; it was her choice to make and her life to live.

Roger didn't like her naturally curly hair either, telling her to straighten it. She did a few times before the chemicals damaged her hair and it started falling out. Nina was done changing herself to suit someone else. She just wanted to be Nina, and if she wanted to wear her hair straight, she'd do it because she wanted to, not because a man demanded it.

Looks were only a façade, anyway. Roger had been the preppy boyfriend who seemed perfect on the surface until she peeled off the top layer and discovered the horrid mayhem underneath. He may not have had any visible ink on his body, but his character was blemished with all kinds of monsters.

Nina should thank him. He had inspired her to reclaim and stand up for herself. Another reason why she came to the marketplace today was because she wanted to search for a tattoo artist. Her colleague had told her to browse the artists' booths for inspiration. She'd been itching for a tat but wasn't sure what she should get.

"Only thirty more minutes left, folks. Make sure you take advantage of the class. If you enjoy it, sign up for the full course today!" the rep spoke into the microphone.

The message yanked Nina out of her reverie and back to the present moment. She ran her hand over the white stone on the table. It was smooth like a rock by the river, where water had softened its surface over time. It looked like a real rock, but when she put on gloves, picked up the carving knife, and pressed the blade to the surface, the rock chips fell away as easily as peeling a potato skin.

According to the instructional video, the Stellar Saxum stone had properties that allowed for easy carving. Once the rock had been sculpted, there was a spray that hardened up the stone and protected it from inclement weather. There was even a solar-light component spray that turned the art into a functional lamp.

For advanced students, they could add unique textures to the rock surface. Nina imagined all the homes that could be built with this kind of cutting-edge material on Earth. The foundation and walls of homes could be solar-powered. All the roads could harness solar light. That would have helped her during the winter months. She hated driving in the ice and snow.

Perhaps one day, humans on Earth would catch up to the technology available in Saedo.

Her hand slipped, and the carving tool took out a large chunk from her rock. *Oh, crap.* See? She wasn't crafty at all.

"You can patch it up like this." The teen star-being with spiky hair from the table beside her smiled. He picked up some fallen scraps and patched them on his sculpture like clay. The way he held the carving tool revealed this wasn't his first time.

"Thanks. You're good at this," she said, admiring the skillful way he carved the stone into an interesting face.

"I like making things." He grinned. "My mom and I always come to these free events. You get to take home whatever you make, including the supplies." His mom was chatting with someone from another table.

A sense of renewal overcame her as she recalled this innate feeling that used to sprout in her as a kid. She had believed in magic and the world of limitless possibilities. Like most little girls, she had been wound up in the magic of fairytales and happily-ever-afters. This sense of infinite wonder didn't come around often, but it had returned today.

Make good use of it, Nina.

She grabbed onto the feeling like a newly discovered gem. A beat later, she shuddered from an odd sensation brushing across her cheek, along her neck, and skidding down the length of her spine. She'd never sensed anything like it. Being here in Saedo, where the energies vibrated on an eighth-dimensional matrix, her body became more sensitive to high frequencies. She'd read that Earth existed on a third-dimensional matrix, where the densities made it difficult to feel certain things.

Maybe she was sensing the combined creative energy from everyone in the marketplace.

Inspired to create something extraordinary, she focused on the stone, wanting to make a cool face like the kid. She didn't put too much pressure on herself and lost herself in the fun of it.

When she was done, she stepped back and studied her carving.

Oh. My. God.

Her heart raced, and she glanced around, hoping no one would see what she had created. How in the hell did she do that?

Zeycott's handsome face looked at her. She even sculpted his neck, making a full bust of him. She had only thought about him while she was chipping away. His handsome face relaxed her, making it easy to work. But she hadn't intended to create him at all.

She swiveled the bust around and noticed a geometric etching on the side of his face. She didn't remember carving that in at all. She glanced at her hands and wiggled her fingers. How had she done that? She had no recollection of it.

She'd heard of people who could do that. Artists and musicians who could step into the creative zone where they lost themselves. They became conduits of the energy flowing through them, letting the energy move them instead of the other way around.

She wasn't a musician or an artist, so how did she achieve this? Was it possible to be partially asleep and partially awake while carving?

Nerves stirred in her stomach, and the odd yet warm sensation that had brushed against her cheek earlier returned. This time, its movement was slow and meticulous. It traveled from one cheek to the other, like a series of gentle kisses.

What was happening to her?

Voices erupted in the hallway. She glanced up at the entrance to the conference room. Zeycott stood outside the doors chatting with Tammo, Huelik, and Jarzell, Rita's lover. A powerful magnetic pull kept her gaze on Zeycott. He wore dark high-tech denim and a yellow short-sleeve shirt that showed off the nice cut of his form. She couldn't take her gaze away from his green biceps and colorful tats. His short brown hair had a messy look, which, to her, was perfect.

Her insides flipped and danced. Her skin heated, and for a moment, she was lost in him. Being lost seemed to be the theme today. A female star-being strode by and stopped to chat with the soldiers. She said something that made Zeycott smile.

Nina jerked as though her organs wanted to jump out of her body and onto him, claiming him. *What in the world is going on?*

She wasn't sexually deprived. She hadn't been with a man ever since her breakup with Roger, but still. A girl had ways of pleasuring herself without a man, so why was she reacting to Zeycott like this?

"That looks incredible!" the teen star-being said, yanking Nina away from Zeycott's direction.

His mother agreed, touching Zeycott's face everywhere.

Stop it. Nina wanted to swat her hand away, but manners kept her in place. "Thanks." She grabbed the sculpture and placed him into the bag that was provided to everyone.

Fear pummeled her. *Please don't come over.* What if Zeycott saw this? How would she explain herself?

I've just been thinking about you too damn much. Somehow, you came through my hands. Could anyone sound lamer than her?

He had never paid any attention to her before. Maybe he wouldn't stop by. *But what if he does?* Seeing a random sculpture of him would bring out a lot of questions she didn't want to answer.

Okay, she had a crush on him, but so did many other females. Like the group who just walked past him and swept their gazes up and down his body as they whispered to each other. There was no law against having crushes. Besides, she wasn't ready to admit anything to anyone yet. She was just having fun, learning a new skill to broaden her horizons. It wasn't her fault if she happened to create a beautiful bust of a man without her intention.

Not too long ago, Sasha had a massive crush on Maeson, so her courageous sister went to track him down, demanding to know why he had stopped talking to her. They made up and fell in love.

Nina's crush wasn't the same, though. The difference being that Sasha and Maeson were already talking to each other, and there had been obvious chemistry between them. So when work took him away, and he never mentioned it to her, she chased him down.

Nina and Zeycott had never spoken. A cordial greeting here and there didn't exactly constitute a conversation or anything. He had never really acknowledged her. Maybe that was because gorgeous female star-beings were always around him.

As she cleaned up the table, something pulled at her, forcing her to glance up. From the entrance, Zeycott stared at her, and pain tugged at his face. It literally strained him, with his eyebrows bunching together and his lips curling as he winced. She supposed he did notice her, just not with the kind of attention she expected or wanted.

Sheesh. Was she *that* unattractive? When she was still living on Earth, men had gone after her. Maybe she didn't fall into Zeycott's category of hot females, but she wasn't atrocious. Well, Mr. I'm-Too-Hot-And-I-Know-It could take his fine face and leave.

Even as she thought that, her body tingled from his intense gaze. Why was he still looking at her?

"Nina!" Jarzell strode through the door, heading toward her. "What are you doing here?"

To her surprise, Zeycott followed him in.

TWO

Jarzell walked up to the table while Zeycott kept his distance by standing a few feet back. He winced, glanced at his calf, and winced again as though excruciating pain was piercing through him. His gaze switched from her to his calf as though she was responsible for his agony. It was almost comical. A few days from now, maybe she'd look back at this moment and laugh at how absurd it was.

Seriously, was she that unattractive?

Nina dragged the bag with the sculpture off the table and placed it on the floor, hiding it from view. "Oh, just learning a new skill. There was a free stone carving class."

"She did an amazing job too," the mother of the teen boy said. "He's hot."

Shush! No one asked for your opinion. She wasn't in the mood for any teasing, even if it was harmless.

Maybe she should go home and take the carving tool to destroy his face and decorate it with tiny holes, so she didn't have to stare at him.

She could feel his stare from where he stood, even though

she wasn't looking straight at him. She saw him in the corner of her eye. Zeycott's gaze singed her skin. How could she react to him like she wanted him when all he displayed was apprehension? Perhaps they were opposites.

"They're just being nice." Nina smiled at the mother. Her son had returned to his unique sculpture of some creature. She needed to change the subject. "What are *you* doing here?"

Jarzell's face turned serious. "The Defendums, our flying droids, picked up a foreign energy around here, so we came to check it out. It seems to have vanished, though." He glanced around the room. "Have you noticed anything out of the ordinary?"

Nina shook her head. "You think the Ulkrins are back at it again already?"

The Ulkrins had attacked Saedo's villages only two weeks ago. Before that, they had sent an energy storm that destroyed several homes and businesses. The villagers were still busy rebuilding from the damages.

These nasty aliens lived in the Province of Agarrek and were known for their malice. They were the monsters who had abducted Nina and her sisters while they had been on vacation. If the soldiers of Saedo hadn't rescued the Nelson sisters, they would either be dead or giving birth to terrifying aliens right now. At that time, Nina and her sisters desperately wanted a new beginning and got that chance when the citizens of Saedo welcomed them.

Many of her sisters had found love with a soldier. Nina was probably going to be the last one. Love wasn't her priority at the moment, but she could find star-beings attractive without thinking about love. Love required a lot more. Right now, she only had room for simple attraction.

In order to love someone, she had to first know herself and what she wanted in life. At the moment, she valued the freedom to do whatever her heart desired.

I deserve a man who loves me and supports my sense of exploration.

She had tossed out that wish into the Universe on that fateful night. All of her sisters had sent a wish of their own as well. Emma, Sasha, Inga, Vanessa, and Rita had their dreams come true in Saedo. Nina was happy for them. The Universe had heard their prayers and answered them.

You can take your time with mine, she told the Universe.

Tammo and Huelik joined Zeycott and whispered something to him. Then they exited the room, leaving Jarzell behind.

Jarzell continued talking to her, "We killed a lot of Ulkrin beasts and their hybrid creatures in the last battle. They're going to retaliate. We've stationed more guards along the borders. Be extra careful when you're out. If you see anything that's abnormal, call the emergency number."

"I will." Nina had been extra careful, not going out at night at all. "Do you have a plan in place? Is there anything I can do to help?"

He smiled, and she could see why Rita fell in love with him. "We do. I'm going to tell you what I tell Rita every time she asks me: don't worry about it. I don't want my woman to live in fear. You're her sister, so that applies to you too."

Nina grinned. "Rita says you're overprotective."

"I can't help it. She matters to me." His eyes brightened every time he mentioned Rita.

Nina wondered if she'd ever find a man who spoke about her in the same way.

Something buzzed on his black metal wristband. "I've got to go now. Don't stay out too late."

"I won't." It wasn't even that late.

A few minutes later, Nina had packed her stuff, thanked Mikasso, and headed toward her next adventure.

She would not let one little mishap ruin her day. Just because Zeycott looked like he was suffering when he saw her didn't mean it affected her.

Yeah, right. Who was she kidding? It crushed her. No girl wanted to be dismissed by the opposite sex like that. Especially one who had occupied her thoughts in more ways than she'd like to admit. She was a strong woman, but she also had feelings.

It was time to shove him out of her mind. One way to do that would require pain. It seemed being lost and in "pain" were the themes of the day.

She was going to get her first tattoo to symbolize a new beginning for her.

Now, what should she get?

THREE

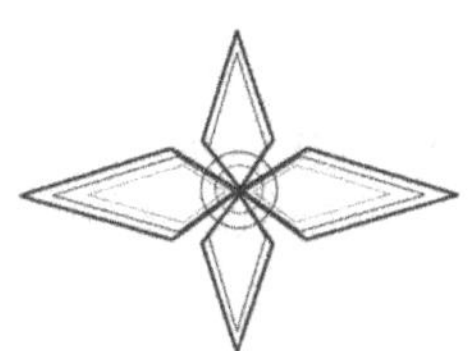

With her shoulder bag and the bust-that-shall-not-be-named in tow, she stopped by the section in the Marketplace reserved for StoryArt Gallery. Unlike before, the room wasn't packed with spectators. She gasped when she saw *The Love Story of Smoke & Mist* hanging on one wall. The smoke and mist in Rita's recent painting collection mesmerized her.

Nina would be thrilled to have an ounce of Rita's artistic talent. The colorful paints moved gently around the framed canvas. Depending on where she stood, the abstraction took on a new appearance. She saw landscapes and faces of various beings that looked holographic. She lifted her hand with the smart ring, snapped a selfie with Rita's painting in the background, and sent it to her sister.

Look what I stumbled on. Congratulations!

A few seconds later, Rita replied, *Thank you!* Followed by a bunch of happy emojis.

Nina browsed the other artwork and stopped by a skeleton of some animal she didn't recognize. Some of its bones had intricate carvings. A sliver of orange mist appeared out of nowhere and flowed around her and the bones. Nina glanced around, looking for its source. Most of the spectators had left except two star-beings that didn't have any orange mist emerging from them.

She recalled her siblings talking about seeing the mist of their forever mates. When that phenomenon occurred, it confirmed they were meant for each other. It was an interesting concept, but she didn't know how she felt about it.

Did the *mist* choose the mate? Or did the *mate* choose his or her lover and the emergence of the mist was just an aftereffect? Like the perfect result of two ingredients that blended well together. She'd find out when her time came.

The orange mist had disappeared by the time Nina left the gallery. She spent another minute viewing other pieces, but nothing inspired her to get a tattoo.

The tattoo shop must have some designs I can pick from.

She pulled up a virtual screen and searched for the closest tattoo parlor. So many options popped up for her to review. She didn't want to go too far away from the Main Village, where she lived. Saedo consisted of several villages, and the Main Village was like a large suburb, and she lived in the downtown area called the Village Center. The closest tattoo shop to her was Versatile Ink.

She slid into her white personal rider—a sleek automobile that moved with swiftness and hovered above the ground. It didn't take her long to adjust to driving one of these state-of-the-art automobiles. They were similar to the sedans on Earth, but these functioned on solar energy, which came in abundance because of the two suns, which also charged her smart ring. The rider could also hover above the ground, which helped her avoid pot holes or anything disrupting her ride.

She glanced up at the sky, which depicted a baby blue color. The delicate color softened the rough edges she'd developed after her encounter with Zeycott. She had a few hours before the suns set. Jarzell's caution about not being out too late echoed in her ears. If the tattoo parlor was too busy, she'd come back another day. She wanted to be home before it got dark.

As she drove off, she spoke to the virtual assistant wired to her personal rider, "N-4, turn on music. R&B."

"Right away, Nina," the female robotic voice replied. "Anything else I can help you with?"

"No, thank you, N-4."

"Have a lovely day, Nina."

Nina pulled into the last parking spot in front of Versatile Ink and got out. The shop was part of a business complex filled with various storefronts. Excitement burst in her when she noticed a fitness studio two doors down from the tattoo parlor. A sign called to her.

Flying yoga! Free First Class! No obligations!

She'd been dying to take this class. As a yogi, she had tried various styles of yoga from Ashtanga, Hatha, Flow, Power, Hot, Vinyasa, to Kundalini. There were a few others, but these were her favorite ones. Lately, she'd been doing more Kundalini to help with her healing process. Yoga could release all the "old" energy that no longer sustained her.

But flying yoga? That was unique to Saedo, and she had to try it. All the other studios that offered this class were in other villages and required a month's commitment. She didn't want to commit to something if she didn't like the first class. This was her chance to try it out with no obligations.

How did she not know about this little gem of a shopping center? She snapped an image of the contact info and saved it to her smart ring so she could sign up later when she got home. It was something to look forward to.

Nina walked up to Versatile Ink, which took up about three times the space of the other shops. The door slid open, and she stepped aside as two red-haired female star-beings exited the parlor. They had light green skin, curvy figures, sexy legs, and boobs that almost spilled over their low-neck-line T-shirts. The breasts appeared abnormally large for their figures; they almost looked like aliens themselves when they jiggled every time the females laughed or moved.

Apparently, star-beings had this breast enhancement device called the manippleator. It injected tiny air bubbles infused with special augmenting enzymes into the breast via a laser beam. The air bubbles were programmed to expand to a certain size once they settled into the tissues, kind of like air bubbles that a remote control could inflate. The patient could also choose the softness level of the newly added tissues as though they were picking out the firmness of the mattress. Not only that, but these enzymes could also balance hormones and blood flow around the chest area, and thus prevent breast cancer and other diseases.

The same applied to those who wanted to reduce the size of their breasts. The enzymes zapped unwanted tissues and marked them as "waste" for the body to excrete them. She'd spent a few days watching this documentary where they had interviewed a few candidates who won a free makeover. These aliens had some wild shows that she'd learned a lot from. The beauty industry on Earth would go crazy about this stuff.

Breast augmentation wasn't as dangerous on this planet as it was on Earth, but it was just as expensive. Who wanted to use their hard-earned credits for a third, fourth, or even fifth breast? Yeah, they had that option available too. Nina wasn't interested in *any* of that.

Nope. No, thank you.

She only found this cutting-edge technique fascinating, especially the mamscan—a high-tech mammogram machine that didn't painfully squeeze the breasts and nipples. It could perform a quick scan with the clothes still on the body. She could imagine all the women rejoicing on Earth.

Nina glanced down at her bosom, which ranged between a B and C cup, depending on the time of the month. She was happy with what God had given her. The female star-beings didn't seem to notice Nina as they walked away, giggling and jiggling.

"He's sooo hot." The female with the yellow T-shirt lifted her forearm and patted the floral design that had a sheen of protection over it. "I'm gonna come back and have him ink my ass. I want those hands on me."

"I can't believe you asked him out." The star-being with the pink T-shirt and matching pink snake earrings elbowed her friend.

"He turned me down, though."

"He owns the place." Pink Snake dug into her purse. "If he went out with every female who wanted a date, it would look bad for his business."

"But he makes me so horny. Anyway, let's go shopping."

The female star-beings strode into a boutique shop.

Nina stepped inside Versatile Ink and noticed two female star beings sitting on metal chairs in the waiting area while watching something on their virtual screens. The shop was spacious, but it didn't reflect the height or the large scale she had observed from the outside. Maybe he used the rest of the space for storage.

She walked up to the reception area where a pink-skinned star-being with tower-high green hair toweled off the marble counter. Something pulled Nina's attention away from the receptionist, and she turned toward a room to her right. She met Zeycott's gaze, and her heart pounded.

He stood like a warrior, pinning her in place with his intense stare, chiseled jaw, and gorgeous midnight hair. Her body became so aware of him that her skin prickled from her neck down to her toes. Her core tightened as though saying hello. He wore the same dark denim she'd seen at the market-place, but his top had changed to a black knit shirt with a swirly logo of Versatile Ink. The shirt illustrated the taut landscape of his muscles, making her swallow the saliva pooling in her mouth.

She wasn't immune to beautiful men, and Zeycott was a fine example of God's work on the male gender.

He didn't look distressed like he did earlier. He turned and said something to someone in the room with him. A female star-being wearing a dress appeared from the room, and he escorted her out to the main area.

"Thank you for the animal tat, Zeycott. I love it." The female star-being gave him a hug.

"You're welcome." He returned the embrace, and Nina's stomach turned.

Why was she even jealous? Nina and Zeycott weren't

dating. They weren't *anything*. She should remember the pain on his face from earlier. *He thinks you're horrid.*

This strange attraction to him confused her. It should have stopped the moment she discovered his harsh reaction to her. There wouldn't be any relationship. There couldn't be. She could never be with a man who didn't love or respect her. Those days were gone. Maybe this was some kind of test from the Universe to see how strong her will was.

Nina had to figure out a way to push him out of her system once and for all.

FOUR

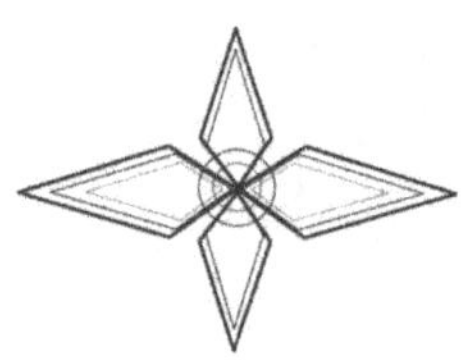

Zeycott walked up to the front desk and stood beside Nina. Energy hummed between them. She sensed the vibration in her bones—which she knew was all in her head. Her body was so sensitive to him. If he simply brushed her with his arm, she'd probably melt into a puddle on the floor.

"Hi, Nina," he said. The way he said her name made her inner thighs quiver.

Nina's lips froze while she shuffled her brain back into its dock.

"Are you getting a tat?" he asked, probably wondering what was wrong with her.

He had the most intense eyes, mostly sage with spears of electric blue bursting from the pupils. The colors pulled at her as though inviting her into some secret world.

How could Zeycott make her feel this way when she hardly knew him? Why should she feel this way when he wasn't interested? *What's wrong with me?*

She didn't like that someone had this much power over

her. Wasn't that the reason her previous relationship had failed?

Her brain finally working again, she replied, "Umm . . . yes. A tattoo. I don't have an appointment, though. Is that okay? I can come back if there's no spot available."

"Kenner just had a cancellation, so he's available," the receptionist said, swiping at the virtual appointment book.

"No. Put her on my schedule, Elleo," Zeycott replied too quickly.

Or had that been her imagination?

"Okay, but I thought you had to leave early today."

"Not anymore." He flicked a glance at Nina. "You'll be my last client today."

He turned, waved at a male star-being with neon blue hair, and they walked together into his studio.

Nina wasn't sure what to feel. Should she jump with glee, or worry that he had a separate agenda? The man who had shown disgust earlier seemed like a different person than the man who appeared to take an interest in her now. Did he shift his schedule around to make time for her?

Maybe he's just being nice. After all, she was the sister to his brothers' significant others.

That had to be the reason because the idea of Zeycott being interested was like coming face-to-face with a flying three-headed pig with polka dot skin. She almost took it back because that animal could very well exist on this planet.

How many times had she daydreamed about him when she was working at Compact Fitness Center? Too many. He'd popped into her head and distracted her during her yoga classes, her cardio workout, and her crunches. With every squeeze of her abdominal muscles, she had imagined squeezing him out of her mind.

It hadn't worked.

It appeared the more she didn't want to bump into him, the more she did. She'd analyze that matter tomorrow. Right now, she had to figure out what kind of tattoo she wanted.

"Hi, Elleo. Do you have a book I can look through for images?"

Elleo smiled, pulled out a tablet from her drawer, and handed it over to Nina. "This one has all of Zeycott's work. You can sort by category, color, or popularity. He also does custom work too. Just ask him."

"Thank you." She was supposed to banish him from her thoughts, not encourage further information about him. Call it morbid curiosity. "Has he been working here long?"

Elleo propped a tattooed arm on her hip. "Honey, he owns this shop. He doesn't work here every day, though. He's also a soldier, so government work takes precedence."

Oh, so he's the one those female star-beings were chatting about.

As Nina swiped through the collection, she ogled his talent. A stream of orange mist appeared and flowed across the tablet. With grace, it moved up her arm and caressed her face. Warmth blossomed, and she recognized the sensation as the one she had sensed at the marketplace.

The sensation had occurred too many times today for her to dismiss it. Fear slithered over her. Seeing the mist for the second time illuminated its significance further. What she had thought was just part of the artwork in the gallery was something more now.

She glanced at the closed door where Zeycott was working. Could he . . . could they . . . be fated?

That was preposterous. Nothing had happened between them that would lead to this development. Could it be a mistake? Was there a lapse or misstep in the mist's lore?

Did Nina conjure up the mist? Was it possible to call on his mist because she had been constantly thinking about him? As a yogi, she understood the power of energy, the power of intention, and how it connected to the mind. Energy flowed with the mind; her mind had been on Zeycott. So, the possibility that she *called* to his mist was high. That was the flow of logic.

Yet she couldn't convince herself to believe anything right now. Because once again, Zeycott had shifted her brain off its dock.

Nerves fluttered in her. Should she be happy that she and Zeycott could be lovers? Did her crazy mind cast some kind of spell without her knowing?

Oh my God. She'd never want to put a spell on someone just so he could like her. She didn't have that kind of insecurity problem.

When Zeycott opened the door to let his client out, she jerked in her chair, almost dropping the tablet.

He met her gaze, and she forgot about the mist and why she had the tablet in her hand.

"You're next," he said.

FIVE

Nina grabbed the bag with the stone bust and ambled into the room with the mist following her inside. Zeycott closed the door behind him.

Stop following me.

Nina Nelson was now talking to a stream of mist. That could only mean one thing. *I've gone insane.*

Ignoring the mist, she focused on the room, which was much bigger than the waiting area. On the other end of the room was a door to an office where she spotted a desk and some bookcases. A small kitchenette decked with fancy appliances gleamed in the corner with two couches. A hallway opened to the right of the kitchen.

"This room is so spacious. It looks homey. Do you . . . live here?" she asked, gesturing to his office.

"Sometimes." He folded himself into the swiveling chair. "Since I own the building, I've set up a little apartment here for convenience. It helps me shift from my soldier duties to tattooing without having to go home."

"I see. Do you love what you do?" Nina placed the tablet down on the counter, and then took off her purse and carefully placed the bag with the sculpture behind it. She couldn't risk him seeing it.

He didn't reply, only stared at her. But the muscle on his cheek twitched as though he were struggling with something.

This could be her opportunity to experiment. If she was the reason for his agony, she wondered how far she could go before he shoved her away. Maybe then her brain and body would let go of Zeycott once and for all.

Yes, that was a brilliant plan, indeed.

Nina walked around his studio, studying the various tattoo art framed on his wall, glanced at the supply cart, and stopped in front of him. She stood close enough that she inhaled a whiff of his musky male scent that made her body almost boneless. Almost. She willed herself to stand straight while her intestines knitted together, churning up more nerves than she expected. Heat raced through her, increasing her body temperature, but she had to keep going. She had to know if he'd push her away. If he couldn't stand her, that would be his only option.

The crease between his eyebrows deepened, and his eyes darkened, then flashed. Did she actually see that? She blinked and looked again. It was probably her imagination. Her gaze flicked to his lips, which were pressed into painfully tight lines. He blew out a ragged breath.

"Are you okay?" she asked as she glanced down his body, trying to see where the agony stemmed from.

He stood steady, so his legs were fine. Maybe it was the tension in his jaw. But her gaze landed on the throbbing vein in his neck. It looked like it wanted to burst from his skin. She went on her tippy toes and leaned in to look, probably a bit too close because she could hear his racing heart.

He veered back. "Are *you* okay?"

The question yanked her eyes to meet his. "Why wouldn't I be?"

"Because you're sweating." His voice grew hoarse.

A bead of sweat slid down from her neck to the center of her bosom. She whipped her gaze down and gasped. Her pink bra was now visible from the wet white T-shirt. From his angle, he could look down and see the perspiration . . . and more.

She wished there was an earthquake that would swallow her up at this moment. Detective work wasn't her forte. She sucked at it.

"Here." He offered her a thick towel from the stack on the table.

She could feel the flames burning in her cheeks and her neck. She wasn't *that* sweaty to need such a thick towel, but she appreciated it. "Thanks." She dabbed her neck, and that was it.

"Do you need some cold water?" A smirk slid onto this face, but he suppressed it. She definitely saw that.

"Y-yes, that would be great. I'm, uh, nervous about getting a tattoo. Never had it done before." She lied and crossed her fingers underneath the towel.

"It's okay." He exchanged the towel with the bottle of blue water.

"Thank you." She gulped it down.

Nina didn't want to make a fool of herself again, so she

wiped the last few minutes from her mind. Now, what had she been thinking before the awful plan of hers took over?

"Why did you choose this profession?" It wasn't any of her business, but it was a safe question that didn't cause her body to heat. He didn't answer right away, and she said, "Sorry, you don't have to—"

"It's a family business. My mother was a tattoo artist as well. She was a lot better than me."

Nina wanted to ask what his mother was doing now, but she decided on a different question. "Do you enjoy this work?"

"I do. It's different from being a soldier. It gives me freedom to create. Versatile Ink has been growing. I want to keep it that way."

"Seems like you're very popular."

"I have two artists working here with me. They have a large clientele."

The orange mist flowed up from his feet, swirled around him, and moved over to her wrist.

Orange mist, go away. It vanished on command.

Something sparked in his eyes, but she could have been *imagining* things again.

A tingle skimmed down her spine, and she couldn't help but feel nervous about the mist or about how her body naturally reacted to him. The potent heat that had made her sweat dimmed a little, but she was still warmer than usual.

He gestured to a metal stool next to him. "Sit. You look nervous. I don't bite."

She snorted. "It didn't seem like that earlier today." *Shit.* She bit her lip, silently cursing herself for not thinking before she spoke.

The spark flashed in his eyes again, making them appear brighter. She hadn't been imagining it earlier. A slight wrinkle formed between his eyebrows but disappeared quickly. He rolled the chair closer to her. "What did it seem like, Nina? Tell me."

Did he know what she was referring to?

The room suddenly felt stuffy, as if the air had left. Her body grew warm with the close proximity to this green man who exuded a powerful magnetism that pulled at her, this handsome star-being who had occupied her mind more than any man.

"Why are there sparks in your eyes? They look like fireworks." She leaned in for a better examination. "Do all star-beings have that ability?"

She hadn't seen any, though. Well, she hadn't been interested in looking that closely at any star-being. Her sisters had mentioned nothing about that when they had their girls' night out. Not that she wanted to hear details about their intimate moments, but she learned each soldier had his own unique trait. Just as each had his own special mist color.

"Answer my question, and I'll answer yours." His voice took on a ragged tone. His hand trembled, but he clenched it into a fist.

He inhaled a breath and closed his eyes. When he exhaled, he opened them. If she didn't know better, she would have thought he was inhaling her scent.

Ridiculous.

Her mind went back to his initial question. *"What did it seem like, Nina?"*

She was tired of making a fool out of herself. Maybe if

she shared her thoughts with him, this infatuation would disappear. There was nothing better than facing her problem directly. Hiding from it hadn't done her any good.

She inhaled and blew out the truth. "You seem . . . disgusted by me. You had this pain on your face when you saw me at the marketplace?"

He flinched from the statement. "No . . . you misread me."

Had she? She knew what she saw.

"Then what was it? You were looking at me, right? Or were you looking at someone else?"

"Oh, I was looking at you." The sage of his eyes brightened, and she could almost see the spark struggling to come through, as though he had stifled it. He raked a hand through his dark mane and blew out a frustrated look. "It's complicated."

"Tell me. I'm all ears. Before living in Saedo, unimaginable things would have shocked me. But after being rescued from monsters and living among star-beings I didn't know existed, 'complicated' has become a subtle word in my dictionary."

He stared at her for a while. Each second seemed to make the room smaller and smaller until she could hear her heartbeat—and his.

No . . . that couldn't be possible.

Zeycott grabbed her hand, and energy snapped upon contact. A burst of colors swirled around them.

"Whoa." Her gaze followed the snapping colors that looked like a little fireworks show. "I'm not imagining this, am I?"

"No, you're not."

"What is it?" Nina waved her hand through the tiny sparks.

"Extreme attraction."

Her eyebrows lifted with amusement. "What did you say?"

His expression didn't show any amusement. "I'm attracted to you."

She couldn't believe it. "Since when?"

"Does it matter?"

"Yes!"

He sat back in his chair, broke the skin-to-skin contact, and the sparks faded. He crossed his arms over his chest, while keeping his gaze on her. "Since my brothers and I rescued you."

Oh. Did he have a secret device that read her thoughts and was now teasing her in the most awful way? If so, she'd kill him.

"Then why didn't you say anything? I hardly saw you around. You didn't attend many parties at Raeko and Emma's house, or at Inga and Osayik's either." She flipped through her mind. She saw him when he had helped Arkon renovate Vanessa's restaurant, Trust Your Gut, and when he had helped Maeson with the back deck.

"I saw you a few times. The most recent was at Rita and Jarzell's, two weeks ago."

She didn't consider that encounter valid. "You didn't stay long. You left right after I arrived."

"I had my reasons."

"I thought you had a mate waiting for you at home," Nina confessed.

His eyes sparked again, this time there was a loud hissing sound. "No, I don't." A pause, then, "I'm not with anyone."

There was something he wasn't telling her. "Why are you telling me this now?"

"Because I'm tired of denying something that makes my heart pound." Zeycott took her hand in his, and energy hissed again, but it was milder this time, as though his energy had gotten familiar with hers. He rubbed a circular motion on the top of her hand with his thumb. Then his attention went to her hair.

"I've dreamed of playing with these brown curls." He threaded his fingers through her long hair. "So soft, so beautiful."

The sounds of their heartbeats thrummed in the room. It seemed distant, and at the same time, close by. She tried to grasp the concept but decided why dissect the rarity of it when she could just dwell in its magic.

Hearing his heart beat along with hers was taking intimacy to a profound level. She still didn't quite understand why he had to hold back. She supposed he could have asked her the same question. Her answer would have been because she feared he'd reject her, so she'd rather keep fantasizing about him.

A part of her rejoiced that he didn't ask. Questions would lead to more questions, and she wasn't ready to talk about her past. Not yet.

"I answered your question—now you can answer mine. Do all star-beings have that spark in their eyes?" Nina cupped the side of his face with each hand, holding him still as she stared into those sage-colored eyes. Electric blue burst like a series of lightning around his pupil. His eyes were like worlds of their own. She wanted to step into their mysteries and unravel him.

"There are other star-beings who have sparks in their eyes. Probably a different color. Everyone's different." His words were almost mumbled. She looked at his lips and realized she had squished his cheeks to where his lips had formed a sexy pout.

She quickly released her palms from his face. "Sorry."

"It's okay. I like your hands on me. And I especially like how you look at me." He smiled, and her stomach churned as though it was forming something delicious inside her. She'd never been mesmerized with laugh lines around the mouth until him.

I'd like your hands on me too. And I love how you look at me now.

"So their eyes can spark like yours too? It's so fascinating."

"They can, but mine are . . ."

She waited for him to continue. "Are what?"

He shook his head. "Nothing. I can get lost in your eyes too."

What was he hiding? Everyone had secrets, and she wouldn't pry if he didn't want to tell her. She hoped that when he got more comfortable with her, he'd share.

A knock sounded on the door and popped the magical bubble encasing them.

Zeycott rose from his seat and opened the door to find Elleo, who had her purse on. No one appeared to be sitting in the waiting room either, and most of the lights had been turned off.

"Just wanted to say good night and let you know that you're locking up. See you tomorrow."

"Good night. Thanks for all your help. Did Kenner leave already?" Zeycott asked.

"Yup. He had a date. He told me to tell you good night as well."

She waved at Nina, and Nina returned the gesture.

Nina pulled up a screen from her smart ring for the time and gasped. It was seven in the evening!

"Oh my God, how did that happen?" How could time fly that fast? It didn't seem like she'd been in the studio room for three hours.

He leaned against the door, looking all smug. "That's what happens when you're in good company."

"I didn't even start my tattoo."

"You could always come back. Do you know what you want?"

Nina shook her head. "It was probably a sign that I'm not meant to get one today."

"There are several reasons to get a tattoo. Some want it for the art. Some want it for symbolism, and others want it to commemorate a loved one. What's your reason? If you can't answer that, then I suggest you wait until you know. Once you know, then it's easy to find the art. I don't want you to pick something and regret it later."

"You're right. I heard that unlike tattoos on Earth, the ink options here can be removed easily?"

"They can. We have temporary ink that disappears after a month. We also have permanent ones. Regardless, getting a tattoo changes the properties of your skin. The effects are different for everyone. I've seen skin lose its softness, natural color, and texture. When you put stuff into your body that wasn't present at birth, it changes the chemistry of your body. Some people don't care. But I think you do."

He was right again. She should have thought about it a lot more before going gung-ho about it. A sense of exploration wasn't a good enough reason to get a tattoo, was it? That spontaneity reminded her of her teen years when she jumped at things without considering the consequences.

Having a sense of adventure could still include a tattoo, but Nina wanted to be sure. There was no one here telling her what to do. No Roger to compete with her. Not that he would in the tattoo area. He wasn't a tat kind of guy.

Though she didn't get her tattoo today, she gained a fresh adventure. Zeycott admitted his attraction to her.

He offered her his hand. "Let's get you home."

She grabbed her purse, picked up the bag that contained his sculpture, and followed him out to the main area. "I didn't mean to stay out so late today. Jarzell warned me about the danger."

"He's right. The villages close their shops early these days. We're doing our best trying to deal with the Ulkrin problem. I'm meeting my brothers tomorrow. They extracted something valuable from the squirmur's brain. I'd like to come see you after that. Would that be okay?"

It's more than okay, stud muffin.

"Okay," she said.

Zeycott's eyes sparked, and something silvery flashed on the wall behind him, but it disappeared after a blink. She turned to meet his sage-colored eyes. Heat pooled at her center from the intense look on his face. There was something else there, but she couldn't tell.

She had Zeycott all to herself in this room. The energy between them heightened and crackled.

"Umm . . . did you hear that?" she asked.

"Yes." His voice was a low rumble of seduction. "Let's get you home before you get yourself into trouble." He ushered her out the door, locked it up, and walked her to her personal rider.

Nina laughed. "What trouble would that be?"

"Me."

Her legs weakened at the thought of her getting into "trouble" with him.

"I'll escort you back home," he said, gesturing to the silver sports rider at the end of the parking lot.

"Oh, you don't need to."

"I want to. It'll make me feel better. Let's exchange contact info." He tapped his wristband to her smart ring.

As she drove home, Nina replayed the day in her mind. Her day had completely changed since this morning. She went from secretly crushing on Zeycott to finding out that he had feelings for her. On top of that, she discovered that she—the simple woman who'd never had much luck with guys—was the *reason* for the sparks in his eyes.

She'd be thinking about this all night. She glanced at the virtual screen that displayed the camera from the back of her rider. It showed Zeycott trailing behind her. Her attention went to the orange mist that appeared in her rider. It swirled in the passenger seat with silver sparkles. For a moment, she thought the mist formed a wolfish face with silver eyes.

Her heart hammered at the sight, and goosebumps bloomed on her neck. Seeing the mist move like clouds was one thing, but seeing a face was another. Unlike Vanessa, who could see spirits, Nina couldn't until tonight. She gripped her hands on the steering wheel and kept her face forward, while trying to see if it was still there. It wasn't.

She definitely saw the face. It wasn't her imagination.

What was it trying to tell her? Was this a different kind of mist and not the one from Zeycott? Had she been seeing someone else's mist? Or was a spirit haunting her?

SIX

The next day, Nina took out the sculpture of Zeycott out of the bag and hid it inside her cabinet. She wasn't ready to show anyone yet.

She kept busy recording videos for her virtual channel, Dexterity Yoga. She started it after one of her clients suggested she could reach a wider audience through the Galacto Net and earn more credits. At first, she'd dismissed the idea because she didn't even have a social media following on Earth. Why would aliens be interested in her yoga videos?

However, being on a new planet allowed her to think differently. She had nothing to lose, so she searched up some popular yoga instructors that had a wide audience and studied them. They had poses she didn't have names for. It fascinated her when she watched videos that showed scaly humanoids and multi-headed creatures with several limbs showing something that looked like the warrior pose.

After watching and studying these well-known instructors, Nina gave it a shot. Why not, right? This was her new beginning, where possibilities were endless.

Dexterity Yoga was still in the beginning stages, but the project excited her. She'd been playing with several ideas to broaden her audience. This was more than having her own yoga channel. This was about making a name for herself, doing what made her heart and soul happy without knowing if it would be successful. It both terrified and excited her.

She was creating her own yoga that resonated with star-beings. How cool was that?

She was grateful to the owner, Soah, for giving Nina a job at Compact Fitness Center when she and her sisters stayed in Saedo to start a new life. She loved her job, but the idea of creating her own hours in her home studio delighted her more. She wanted to be her own boss.

Nina checked on the videos she had uploaded yesterday, including the class she'd offered for a small fee, and blinked at the subscribers. Holy cow! She had gained two hundred thousand subscribers in a single day! She closed her eyes, breathed, then opened them to look again. Nope, it wasn't her imagination at all. She had gained another ten from the few seconds when she had her eyes closed.

She read some of the comments.

We want more!

Outstanding poses!

What is that pose called?

We love your style. So peaceful.

Just purchased your yoga class! Love it so far!

Her smile widened, and she did her best to reply to comments and questions.

Maybe the overnight success was because she was one of

the few humans offering various yoga methods. She didn't stick to a particular style. For her, the mood dictated the style.

Taking the week off had been a fantastic idea. She could spend more time making more videos. But first, she needed some self-care, and that meant a yoga session for herself. She situated herself in the middle of her living room and performed a short yoga routine.

During the last few breaths of meditation, Zeycott's face flowed into her mind like a breath of fresh air that revitalized her body. Then her mind dove into a sinful adventure where she demonstrated the poses for him in the nude. Desire coursed through her, making her body all warm. She shook her head and cursed herself for digressing.

Focus, Nina. You have work to do.

She rose and gulped down a bottle of blue water infused with tiny crystals. If she wanted to get all the recordings done today—or at least the next months' worth—then she needed to stay in her lane and stop her mind from wandering into Zeycott territory.

Nina ambled over to the camera on the robotic tripod and adjusted the light lens settings. She preferred soft lighting to achieve a certain mood. She had a few peaceful backdrops in mind that would complement the mood she wanted. She'd decide on that later.

When that camera was all set, Nina went over to her silver-metal droid with glowing blue eyes.

"How are you today, Nina? What can I do for you? Video recording or cleaning the house?" asked Lorinz, who was her personal assistant with many skills.

"I'm well, thanks. I'd like your help with video recording

today. A three-sixty to capture all angles would be great." She tapped his arm.

"You got it." He nodded and his blue eyes glowed.

She pressed a button on his chest and programmed him to do an overall view that would capture the angles a stand-still camera wouldn't get. He'd turn on the camera embedded in his forehead while walking around her during the poses.

She loved her work and her mission to connect to the body, mind, and spirit. She believed in it because it had healed her. More than anything, yoga had helped her maintain the carefree spirit and her desire for exploration.

Looking back, Roger had almost destroyed that part of her. Love was an interesting thing. Its serrated edges could cut deeply. But that was because she had chosen the wrong man.

Live and learn.

If only Roger could see what she was doing now, he'd flip. He'd fume about her large following just because he could. He had never wanted to see her succeed. By keeping her down, he would always be "better." She never understood the insecurity in him. He even envied his own brother and sister, so it shouldn't have been a surprise that he had treated her the way he did.

Love had cast its own deceptive lenses over her eyes, making her see things that weren't true. But everyone succumbed to that weakness at least once in their life. At least that was what she concluded after talking to some friends and coworkers.

A part of her feared this powerful attraction to Zeycott. Was she seeing an illusion? Was she *feeling* the truth? It was hard to tell when she was so wrapped up in him. She'd never been this attracted to anyone. Her body yearned for him in ways she couldn't explain.

Be careful, Nina. Beautiful things can still be dangerous.

Her chest constricted, and she placed a hand over her racing heart.

She turned to her droid. "Protect your heart—your corra. No one else is going to do that for you. Right, Lorinz?"

"It is a vital organ that needs protection, Nina. You have a beautiful one," Lorinz spoke in his robotic voice.

Even though Lorinz was a droid, the emotions programmed into him made him real to her. All metal, he stood seven feet tall, and his arms and legs could extend to unimaginable lengths. He also possessed strength that was useful when she had heavy things to cart around. His skills also included cleaning the house.

When she was on Earth, she couldn't afford cleaning services. Besides, she didn't trust anyone enough to have them in her home when she wasn't around. But she trusted Lorinz because she could program him to do whatever she needed. All she had to do was insert the appropriate software into his chest cavity.

When she had shopped for a droid, she wanted one that looked like a star-being in the flesh. Those were high-end droids she couldn't afford. She chose Lorinz because he fell into her range of affordability, and that made him cuter. A week after she brought him home, he became her friend.

After a few hours of recordings, she deactivated Lorinz to let him rest. Yesterday, while she was out, he'd cleaned the house and used up a lot of stored energy. He needed to recharge from the crystal charger because she had stuff to do tomorrow.

Nina sat down at her computer to review her work. She trimmed some videos, cut, and pasted scenes for a seamless flow. She sorted through her collection of background displays that ranged from a peaceful beach, relaxing forest, to breathtaking mountain sceneries. Then she incorporated the instructions with her voice and soft instrumental music. She scheduled two yoga video sessions to go live on her channel a few days apart. Then she added a third video where they had to pay to watch.

Her smart ring buzzed, and a message from Zeycott splashed on her virtual screen.

Z: See you around five. What are you doing?

Her body shuddered from his message. Did he know she had been thinking about him? Had he been thinking about her too?

N: Just finished up with yoga. What are you doing?

Z: Thinking of you and yoga. Downward dog appeals to me. Show me sometime?

She gaped at the message. A flurry of sensation zipped down her body as she envisioned him imagining her in yoga poses—some of which could be sexual positions. Yes, she had thought about that several times.

N: Okay, but I want to see your tattoos. Fair trade?

Though she had seen his ink from afar when he had worked on Maeson's house, she wanted a close-up. Details mattered.

Z: Deal. Did you have lunch yet?

She glanced at the digital clock embedded in the wall. She'd forgotten to eat again. On days when she worked at home—two days out of the week—she often missed lunch because she lost track of time. Despite that, she favored the flexibility of working from home. One day, she could afford it.

N: *I will.*

She loved the simple conversation between them, even if it was only text messages. There was no awkwardness. If there were any pauses, they were mostly from her, taking a moment to blush and gather herself. She had blushed more with him than anyone else.

N: *How was your meeting? Any news about the Ulkrins?*

Z: *Yes. Very helpful. There's a yoga studio near my shop. Heard good things about it.*

N: *Wanna try flying yoga with me?*

Z: *Flying yoga? What's that?*

N: *Supposed to be good for your lymphatic system. There's a free class.*

Z: *Umm. . .*

N: *It's OK if you're scared. This is your chance to see me in poses.*

Z: *Only if you promise not to laugh.*

N: *Promise.*

Z: *Don't mention this to your sisters. If word gets to my brothers, I'll deny knowing anything about flying yoga.*

Nina couldn't help the giggle that burst from her.

N: *I'll catch you if you fall.*

Z: *(smiling emoji)*

N: *(emoji of a female catching a falling star-being and landing with the one-arm superhero pose)*

Z: *(laughing emoji) Gotta go now. Urgent meeting. See you soon. Go eat. (food emoji)*

Her grin widened as she stared at the message box. She couldn't believe he would try flying yoga with her.

The orange mist surfaced from somewhere and flowed in front of her, forming a female face with silvery sparks. Last night, seeing that wolfish face startled her, but she hadn't been afraid. She didn't feel any negative vibrations from the mist. Now it had returned. What did it want from her?

She waved a hand through the misty image, breaking it into wispy slivers. The slivers shifted and returned to form the female face again.

Should she share this with Zeycott? Was it too soon to mention something that might link them together as starmates? Was she ready for the enormous leap?

It was one thing to be lusting after a man who made her want to jump his bones, but it was another thing to be linked to him permanently. *Forever.*

How could she know if this attraction wasn't just a temporary phase that would disappear in a month or so? Sometimes attraction didn't last. She'd experienced that a few times in her life.

"Forever" was a simple word that held so much power. It gave people hope, and at the same time, appeared too unrealistic to grasp.

Every girl wanted to find a forever mate, someone who was her equal. Someone who loved her unconditionally.

I deserve a man who loves me and supports my sense of exploration.

Her wish to the Universe echoed in her mind.

This was a serious matter that needed careful analysis. She'd share it with Zeycott later. For all she knew, this orange mist could signify something totally different. It first emerged at the marketplace when she was looking at various sculptures and installations. He hadn't even been around. She didn't want to discuss something that could end up meaning nothing.

Besides, she wanted to know how he felt, regardless of the mist. That was more important than any myth.

These inquiries needed some insight. Grandma Ova popped into her mind. It was time for Nina to make a visit. She'd heard so much about this wise woman from her sisters. But Nina hadn't had a reason to discuss anything with her except that one time Nina encountered her at the Galactic Galleria, a large grocery store in the Village Center. Grandma Ova had shown up for a special vendor event. That had been the first time Nina tried Grandma Ova's herbal soup made from vegetables and herbs in her garden. The soup had a hint of sweetness and spices that settled her stomach and released toxins gently. Her body always felt lighter after eating that cleansing soup.

She wished she had some of it in her icebox. That would have been a great lunch. Instead, she settled for some leftovers of the Nelson meat pie, which was Vanessa's version of a shepherd's pie, and a container of chanterelle mushrooms, which promoted strong hair and nails.

After the quick lunch, she continued working on her videos and drafted an outline for future projects. The hours passed, and before she knew it, the doorbell rang with Zeycott's face splashing on the wall of her security monitor.

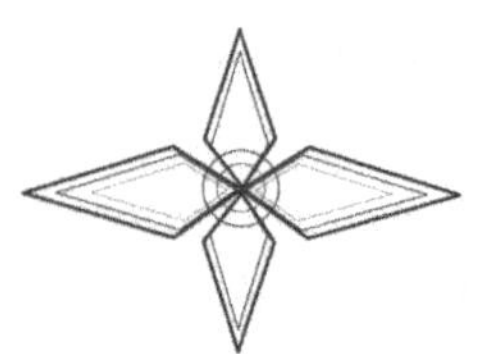

SEVEN

Nina rushed to the door, not caring that she hadn't changed out of the yoga outfit she'd worn for the last recording. She had on some makeup and tightened her ponytail.

She opened the door and smiled. "Good evening."

"Good evening to you too," he said and stepped inside.

He glanced at the spa-like setup she had in her living room, and kicked off his shoes, placing them on the mat by the door. She liked that he was perceptive enough to know that she preferred her space clean. It made working and recording easier. Too much disarray cluttered her energy.

"Dinner for us." He held up a bag from a local restaurant. He wore a button-down blue shirt with the sleeves rolled up past his elbows and the hem tucked inside high-tech denim pants with zipped pockets. She recognized the design as one from Inga's denim collection.

After making a name for herself in Saedo, Inga had expanded her fashion collection to include lingerie, yoga wear, shoes, and accessories. Nina was so proud of her sister.

She deserved her happiness with Osayik, who supported her creative outlet.

"Thanks. You didn't have to." Nina took the bag and placed it on the kitchen counter. "Make yourself at home. I can give you a tour after I take out the food."

"I can give myself a tour."

While she plated the food and brought it over to the kitchen table, Zeycott browsed her apartment. The air in the room pulsed with a sexual energy that swirled around her root chakra, snaked up her spine, and shook her body. This was the Kundalini energy awakening from its coiled spot at the base of her spine, slithering up her body. Kundalini was so much more than sexual force, as most people thought. To Nina, it was more of a spiritual healing process. With her failed relationship, Nina had turned inward, trying to understand herself, and found that the kundalini yoga practice helped her anchor herself more than the other styles. There was no manual to teach someone how to heal themselves, so she had gone with her gut.

Most women experienced kundalini rising in their forties, but Nina was only twenty-six years old. She had acquainted herself with this sexual energy earlier than most. The rise of sexual energy marked a new stage in her life. She had the hots for a star-being.

Zeycott stood staring at Lorinz, who stood immobile against the wall.

"What does he do for you?" Zeycott asked.

"A lot of things. Lorinz is my assistant. He helps me record my yoga videos so I can load them onto the Galacto Net. He does it with minimal errors."

"You have a virtual channel?" His eyes sparked with

interest, and he pulled up a screen on his wristband. "What's it called?"

"Dexterity Yoga."

Her stomach quivered as she watched him *watch* her videos. She'd worn tight clothing while performing poses that heightened the sexual energy in the room.

"And how does *Lorinz* help you?" His lips formed a pout.

She smiled. "He captures all the angles that my other camera can't. And he keeps the house clean for me."

Zeycott's face turned serious. "I'll be your assistant the next time you record."

Was he jealous of a droid?

"I'm sure you're swamped with work for the Saedo government and Versatile Ink. I don't want to intrude."

He tipped up her chin. "I can shuffle my schedule around."

Electric blue sparked within the sage of his eyes. He towered over her by a foot. Heat radiated from his body and clung to hers. Would she be able to concentrate if Zeycott recorded her? Knowing that his eyes would be on her ass and breasts would disrupt her concentration more than anything else. Would she be productive?

Absolutely not.

An image of him touching her while she held seductive poses floated across her mind and made her shiver.

He smirked as though he knew exactly what had gone through her brain at that moment.

Nina traced her fingers along his strong jawline. "You might get bored."

"I assure you; I won't get bored. I'll get to see your body from different angles instead of just *imagining* them."

Heat flushed her face, and her legs felt weak, trying to think of what he had imagined about her.

"I'm sure you get to see a lot of female body parts at your tattoo parlor."

Humans got tattoos on various parts of their bodies, and star-beings were no different. The star-beings had more body parts to ink on, including sensitive areas that made her cringe. She didn't like the thought of him touching another woman intimately, even if it was part of the job.

"It seems like you have some clients who love having your hands on them." She remembered the two female star-beings she had encountered outside of his shop.

One eyebrow quirked. "Are you jealous?"

She countered, "Are *you* jealous of my droid?"

His eyes twinkled. "I think we both know the answer to that." His hand cupped the back of her neck, and energy zipped down her back.

Zeycott scanned her face, lowered his lips, but stopped centimeters away. His breath warmed her skin, and the musky male scent made her body sag into him. His mouth opened slightly, as if to say something. Just one move and his lips would be on hers.

Kiss me.

Zeycott released a breath and winced. Pain washed over his expression. He drew back, creating a wide distance between them. The space turned cold from the separation. She yearned for his closeness again, but the agony on his face hurt her. Was something wrong with her that made him react that way?

"We should eat before the food gets cold," Nina whispered.

Hurt and embarrassed, she turned from him and walked to the kitchen table. She didn't have an appetite, but she needed to do something, needed to keep her hands busy.

"Nina," he called after her, his voice steeped in sadness and regret. "There are some things you don't know about me. I'll tell you when the time is right. For now, let's just enjoy each other's company." She felt the heat of his body behind her.

At least he was being honest with her. The anxiety on his face tore into her as she faced him. She reached up and rubbed the tension between his eyebrows. She desperately wanted to know what was wrong with him. Who had hurt him to where he couldn't even kiss her?

Nina understood that a relationship required patience along with love and honesty. She'd give him the space and time he needed. She could use the time as well. Zeycott had gone from a secret crush to being inside her apartment and jealous of her droid in one day. Slowing down could benefit both of them.

For now, she could settle for his company and learn about him. There would come a day when she'd want more, and she prayed that he'd be ready to give her more.

Nina would not settle for a relationship where the other person wasn't completely truthful to her. She was done with being the only one putting in the effort.

What was complicated about Zeycott's situation?

She sensed a deep wound lurking within him. And like any untreated wound, it could reopen. Most individuals would slap a bandage over it, hoping that temporary fix would be enough. But in truth, the wound needed a better treatment.

Nina had placed several bandages—known as excuses—over the damages caused by Roger. They hadn't healed. Instead, they had festered into something worse.

He didn't mean what he said.

He was just having a bad day. Ignore him.

He hates to lose. I should have let him win. I made him look foolish in front of his friends. I shouldn't have done that.

Excuses could all go to hell now. It was only when she was ready to remove those temporary bandages that she began to truly heal.

Was Nina able to help Zeycott now? Did he even want her to?

"Okay. When you're ready, I'm here." She tabled the concerns and enjoyed his company for the evening.

"When is the flying yoga class?" He folded himself into the chair in the kitchen, looking comfortable, like he belonged in her home. He dug into the food, which consisted of pasta noodles with hematiss-chicken—made from the hematiss plant that mimicked meat—sautéed vegetables, and a side order of pink fries.

Nina pulled up a virtual screen. "Looks like the next available class is three weeks from today. And they only have a few openings left. I'll sign us up now. This will give you some time to prepare yourself."

"Prepare myself?"

"Yeah. If you haven't done yoga in a while, you might be stiff. You won't enjoy the class as much. I can help you acclimate before the class."

"Define 'acclimate.'" He looked at her suspiciously.

Nina laughed. "I promise it's nothing to worry about. You won't pull a muscle or break a bone, but . . ."

"But what?"

"But . . . you'll just have to wait and see."

Oh, she was going to enjoy torturing him for the rest of the evening.

"You're evil." He stabbed the fork into the pasta.

"I'm not. I just don't want you to embarrass yourself during class."

"Why would I embarrass myself?" He narrowed his eyes.

"Well, from my experience of teaching classes on Earth, sometimes men unknowingly joined the class with their significant other. They weren't prepared and 'reacted' unexpectedly to some of the yoga poses."

His eyebrows furrowed, and she sighed. "The poses turned the men on. It was obvious because they were wearing workout pants."

"Ohhh . . ." His eyes gleamed. "That's very nice of you to think in advance." Then he leaned in. "Or are you just trying to get a personal glimpse first?"

Nina rolled her eyes. "As a teacher, I'm trying to save you from humiliation."

"But as a beautiful female who's attracted to me, what are *you* trying to do?"

Trying to make sure other females don't stare at you. Trying to spend more time with you. Lots of things.

But she couldn't share those. *Time to switch topics.*

"Dinner's getting cold. If you don't eat yours, I'll have your portion too."

EIGHT

The next two weeks flew by.

Zeycott started a routine where he would stop by after work and bring her food. They wouldn't discuss anything about the yoga practice, mostly because there was never time after dinner. While they ate and chatted about their day, Zeycott would wince. She could never tell where the discomfort came from. Every time she inquired, he'd say, "I'm fine. Don't worry about it."

Aside from that, all was well. Despite the enjoyable time, there was a vexing undercurrent that worried her. Everything seemed too good to be true.

The day before the flying yoga class, Nina didn't have to work at Compact Fitness Center. She spent the day in casual clothing, editing her yoga videos in her mini-office, which was tucked in the corner of her living room.

Zeycott arrived earlier than usual, wearing a black short-sleeve top and matching loose pants, looking like he'd just gone to the gym. She loved how his green skin contrasted with the dark outfit. She wanted to run her fingers through his messy dark hair. He had a warrior's body, ready to defend and attack when necessary. His biceps and forearms were like weapons at the ready. The tattoos that peeked through the sleeve hems added another layer of danger that made her yearn to see the rest of him.

His eyes blazed through her, igniting something in the pit of her stomach. "I'm ready."

She turned her screen off and studied him some more. "Why are you dressed like this? Did you just come from the gym?"

"I did. I'm preparing for our date tomorrow. You know, the flying yoga class? I'm hoping you will give me some tips. Show me some moves so I don't make a fool out of myself. I thought you were trying to save me from humiliation."

Amused, Nina arched an eyebrow. "That option is available if you're interested. But if you're confident in your skills or don't care what others think, then you don't need the practice."

"I don't want to embarrass *you*. If I'm with a seasoned yoga instructor, then I should at least know *something*, right?"

An old habit rose to the surface. She couldn't help but compare him to Roger. Was Zeycott trying to compete with her? Was he trying to make himself look better?

Someone looking in her brain might consider her thoughts as major insecurities. But for Nina, it was her way of protecting herself. If Zeycott depicted similarities to Roger, then she would have to force herself to end this relationship. It was better to nip it in the bud than let it grow into something monstrous.

But how he worded his concern changed her mind. He

didn't want to embarrass *her*. Roger had never voiced anything that considerate.

Nina got up from her seat and ambled over to where he stood in the middle of the living room. She walked around him, admiring his body. "Does this make you uncomfortable? Me examining you."

"Should it?" He met her eyes. Not a hint of nerves flickered in them.

She tried to see where the pain came from, but she didn't pick up on any. Was the pain random, or did he know exactly when it would emerge? From what she'd observed so far, she concluded it was random.

"I know for a fact that the females in the class will look at you the way I am now. So, if you're uncomfortable, we can practice so you can get comfortable."

A smile touched his lips. "I love how you're *improvising* the lessons."

"That's part of being a seasoned teacher. I adjust according to my client's needs." She placed a hand on his firm chest and felt the thumping of his heart. She swept a quick gaze down his body, looking for signs of twitching.

"I know what you're trying to do," he said. "I can't conjure up the discomfort, Nina. It comes and goes. My body's trying to adjust to the potency."

She pursed her lips. "I want to know what's going on with you. What if you get injured during the class? I don't want that to happen."

He let out a laugh. "I won't. The pain isn't from a muscle." He stroked a finger down her cheek. "I'll tell you soon. I'm waiting for some tests to come back before I share everything with you."

She could deal with that. "Okay."

His eyes bore into hers. "I like how you study me, though. Makes my body come alive." His voice took on a husky tone. "See anything you like?"

"Oh, yes. A lot of things." She tossed him a flirtatious smile. "Give me a few minutes to change, and I'll be right out. You can pick your choice of a mat from over there." She gestured to the bucket with a variety of yoga mats in various colors and patterns.

"Why do you have so many?" he asked, rummaging through her bucket.

"I like pairing the scenic views with an appropriate mat to set the mood. Ambience is important to me. Besides, I don't want to get bored using the same mat over and over. You can settle anywhere on the wooden floor."

Nina went into her bedroom and pulled out three yoga outfits from Inga's new yoga wear collection. They were made from innovative materials that increased her metabolism, relaxed cramped muscles, and absorbed sweat to keep her body dry. In addition, the pores on the fabric provided a boost of oxygen to help with breathwork. These yoga outfits cost a lot of credits, but Inga had given them to Nina for free. Nina wore Inga's yoga wear collection to promote her fashion business while Inga splashed images of Nina's yoga channel on her online store. That was how they helped each other.

Nina stripped out of her T-shirt, bra, and long cotton pants and pulled on a sexy peach top, pairing it with matching floral shorts that had cutouts on the sides, revealing portions of her bare skin to him. She hadn't planned on wearing this outfit for her virtual channel. It was a bit too risqué for public videos, but she could wear it now. She was simply going to torture a stunning star-being who was tormenting her just by standing in her apartment.

Though Nina agreed to give him time regarding his pain, she said nothing about delaying her personal agenda of kissing him. He had been so close to kissing her the other day. How far could she push him today before he broke through his resistance and kissed her?

This was an experiment she was dying to try.

A growl sounded behind her, and she turned around to find Zeycott leaning against the doorframe with his arms crossed over his chest. He wore the charming expression of a male in heat. The cotton pants didn't hide the grand bulge that reflected the lust in his eyes.

Had she forgotten to close her bedroom door?

She cleared her throat. "Don't you knock? How long have you been standing there?"

"Not long. I wanted to ask you something, but your door was open. It's my fault. I took one look and couldn't walk away."

The thought of him watching her made her panties wet. Was it wrong of her to like that idea? What the hell was wrong with her?

She narrowed her eyes. "Do you often watch women get dressed? Some might consider that creepy."

His gaze swept up and down her body. "No. But normal rules don't apply to you. It's not creepy when there's an attraction between us. Seeing you in this way is like watching my fantasies come true."

Zeycott pushed himself away from the doorframe and walked up to her. His gaze landed on her bosom, which looked even more voluptuous from the way the yoga top pushed it up.

"You've fantasized about me?" she asked.

"I'm certain I'm not the only male who has fantasies about you." His hand brushed against her cheek, and energy snapped. "I love how I make you blush." His fingers skimmed along the column of her neck, along her shoulders, and down her arms to intertwine with her fingers.

Her body shivered from the intimacy of their joined hands.

Confusion washed over Nina. Zeycott's actions showed he wanted her, but why hadn't he kissed her?

The idea of breaking his barrier solidified in her mind. *How much do you want me, Zeycott?*

Tonight, she'd get the kiss she'd been craving. If he got to live his fantasy, then she had to have hers too.

"What did you need to ask me?" Nina recalled the reason he came to her bedroom.

"What?" The sage color of his eyes had turned to a dark forest green that spoke of a dangerous desire.

Knowing that she had fogged up his brain, she smiled. "You said that you wanted to ask me something. What did you need?"

"What I need is something I shouldn't have right now." The guttural growl in his voice made her thighs clench.

Nerves continued to dance along her arms.

"I came to ask you which yoga mat you preferred so I could get yours set up. But then I saw you pulling up your pants . . . and I forgot everything else."

"What I need is something I shouldn't have . . ." Maybe he just needed a little nudge.

Nina gripped his hand and led him back out to the living room. "Shall we start?"

"Yup. Show me what I need to know."

"Have you done any yoga at all?" she asked, standing on her green yoga mat, while Zeycott moved to face her on his gray mat.

"A while ago, when I was injured during a mission. I tried some poses that helped stretch out my back and legs, but I haven't done any since."

"We'll start off with the basics. Just mimic my moves. If anything hurts, stop. Don't overdo it."

Nina started off with the sun salutation pose, bringing her palms together at her chest in a prayer mudra. Zeycott repeated her steps successfully.

"Breathe. It's easy to forget. The breath is important," she said and noticed that his arousal hadn't gone down from earlier.

How could he concentrate when his little friend—or rather "big" friend—wanted attention?

Trying her best to ignore Zeycott's rod, Nina came down to a forward bend, with her hands touching the floor for the ultimate leg stretching. As she came back up, she intentionally slowed her movement and offered him a glimpse of her breasts.

You're a naughty girl, Nina.

The boldness surprised her. On a normal day, she wouldn't have done this. She wouldn't have dared. But today wasn't a normal day. Her current life wasn't normal, at least not the definition of "normal" from the dictionary on Earth. She was now living an abnormal life, so unconventional that it opened new doors for her.

Her sense of exploration had shifted when she started living in Saedo. A new planet meant a new identity. She could be and do whatever her heart desired. No one could judge her here. And right now, she wanted to seduce this gorgeous green man who could make her body want more than any other man.

The low neckline of her top gave him a sumptuous view. He sucked in a breath, and when his erection twitched, she smiled. *Victory.*

"Don't tell me you're out of breath already." She sent him a seductive look. Her body grew warm, but not as hot as that time in his tattoo parlor.

He swallowed, and his eyes darkened. "You're evil."

"I don't know what you're talking about. I'm just teaching yoga, which is an exercise that promotes peace of mind. I'm trying to bring you to a meditative state, Zeycott."

"Flekken! Peace of mind, my ass. You're driving me crazy. My brain just dropped in between your breasts. It's now lost in that luscious landscape."

She laughed. "My boobs won't bite. They'll take good care of it, don't you think?"

He cursed again, and the veins on his neck pulsed.

"Please keep in mind that cursing isn't allowed in my yoga classes. Now, follow my directions. Do what I do."

Nina lowered to all fours on the yoga mat and prepared herself for the cat-cow pose. With an inhale, she arched her back and lifted her chin and chest toward the ceiling. With an exhale, she drew her belly in, rounding her back in a cat pose.

She repeated the steps a few times. "This cat-cow pose warms up your body and adds flexibility to the spine."

She flicked a glance his way to make sure he was doing it right. He was on his hands and knees, but he wasn't doing any yoga moves. Instead, he prowled over to her like a wild animal, ready to unleash the dark desires flaring in his eyes.

She sensed the heat pumping off his body. Silver sparks burst from his sage-colored eyes, and he winced. Pain strained his face, and he struggled to fight it.

Concern had her straightening up on her knees. "Are you—"

Zeycott swiftly got on his knees, cupped her face with both hands, and crushed his lips to hers.

The sensation of warm lips ignited a burning flame that sent a powerful jolt through her body. His tongue coaxed her lips open. When they did, he slid in and conquered.

An explosion of colors flashed in her vision. His mouth devoured hers with predatory grace. His hands traveled down to her breasts, capturing and molding them. She felt a rush of tingles skipping down her spine. Her body came alive as though she'd just gotten a boost of energy from some life-inducing drug.

"Nina, you're killing me." He groaned. "But I don't give a shit."

The hunger in his eyes kicked her desire up a notch. She had wanted this kiss, and it was beyond what she had imagined. It was a hundred times better. She had toyed with his will, and she had won.

With eager hands, he removed her top and whipped it aside. Her breasts sprang free for his eyes. His mouth dropped open, and his tongue slid out, performing that savory motion along his lip that made her yearn for him to do that in other areas of her body.

He growled and captured a nipple in his mouth. Sensations rocked her body, and her fingers slid into his hair, tugging. One of his hands kneaded her other breast with soft, rhythmic pressure, while the other hand rounded to her back and claimed her ass. She arched toward his voracious mouth as he lavished attention on her breasts.

"This . . . this wasn't part of the class," she muttered.

"I'm improvising. I'm adjusting to my teacher's needs . . . and my needs," he spoke and blew a cool breath on her nipple before ravaging it again.

She almost laughed at how he'd twisted her words, but her brain couldn't form any logical thoughts. Her body went soft and boneless, molding to the hardness of his form. She was now laying on her mat with his body covering hers. He glanced down, and perspiration glistened on his forehead.

Nina reached up and dragged his mouth to hers. She teased and taunted him, torturing him in the most delicious ways. "I've wanted you for so long."

He caught her earlobe and nibbled. "The feeling is mutual."

His hand wandered down the side of her ribcage, fueling a river of fire with each touch. His hand found its way between her legs, and her legs fell open to him shamelessly.

Zeycott crooned. "You're going to be the end of me." His eyes flashed with wicked desire. "But I'm having you, anyway. Nothing is going to stop me."

"This is just the beginning. Off." Nina tugged at his shirt. "I want to see you too."

His shirt flew off, and her hands roamed all over his gorgeous chest, claiming every muscle she could touch. The green color of his skin fluctuated its shade with her every touch. It became darker, just as his eyes darkened.

Her fingers traced the abstract tattoos on his shoulders and biceps. Before, she had thought they were abstract art. But up close, the tattoos appeared like a series of little images telling a story. Scars—a lot of them—lay underneath the art.

Nina's heart stuttered. "What happened here?"

"A story for another time, beautiful. Don't distract me from having you. It won't work." He yanked her shorts off, including the tiny thong with a single rose covering her center.

"How fitting. My perfect flower." He palmed her wet center, and a finger entered her. "I'm going to make you bloom." A wicked smile stretched across his handsome face, and she wanted to bite him.

With the intense gaze pinning her, he slid in another finger and drove her wild. "Is there a yoga pose name for this?"

She tried to connect to her brain. "No." She breathed, and he drove in deeper. "I mean, yes. The Handyman."

A laugh mixed with a growl escaped him as he curled his fingers, hitting a sensitive spot. Nina cried out in pleasure.

She squirmed under the decadent assault of his fingers and the base of his wide palm. "Zeycott . . ." Her thighs weakened and opened wider for him.

"Flekken, Nina." He crooned like a beast with no control.

He yanked his fingers out of her, and her body disapproved of the void. It bucked, wanting his attention again.

This was the exploration she had been yearning for. To be intimate with a man who made her feel alive. So alive that the gasps and sighs of sex became melodies to a song sung between them. Her heart drummed to the lovely tune. She had never experienced such a deep connection with anyone.

When his lips pressed against her center, pleasure sliced her in half. Sensations whipped her head from side to side. She moaned out some words she didn't understand. Her reaction urged him on. She felt like she was flying somewhere with nothing to hold onto. She sensed the erratic storm gathering inside her and stretched out her hands, trying to grasp something. Nothing was in her reach except the yoga mat. Her body bowed as pleasure coiled.

When the powerful wave of her orgasm ripped through her, her hips thrust into him as her vision burst into a starry bliss. "Zeycott!"

Zeycott continued loving her until his wristband buzzed.

He ignored it once. But the second buzz sounded different. He cursed and lifted his face to hers. "Sorry, I have to take this. It's urgent."

"Okay." Nina breathed. She didn't mind the extra moment to catch her breath. Her body needed time to absorb the magic she'd just experienced.

Zeycott sat up beside her and prepared to return the call.

She propped on an elbow, studying him. Topless, but still wearing his pants. His arousal called to her, and she palmed it. It throbbed in her hand through the fabric.

"If Raeko's call isn't urgent, I'm going to kill him." Zeycott seethed.

"You can chat while I do my thing." She bit her bottom lip. "This pose is called sharpening the staff."

"You're so dirty." He groaned and returned the call with video off.

"It's your fault," she replied as she played with him.

Raeko's name blinked on Zeycott's wristband, signifying the connection. Raeko and her oldest sister, Emma, had fallen in love when he led the soldiers to rescue them.

"Tammo discovered a tunnel," Raeko said. "We're going to check it out. Can you join us? I'm expecting Ulkrins."

The word "Ulkrins" soured the sexy mood, and she sat up. A worry of concern washed over her.

"I'll be there." After he clicked off, he turned to her. "We'll finish this another time." He wrapped an arm around her, pulling her close. "I've never had such an interesting yoga class."

While he got ready to go, she reached for a throw on the couch and covered herself. "Be careful."

He walked over and gave her a kiss on the forehead. "I'm not sure what time I'll be back, but is it okay if I swing by?"

He wanted to stay the night?

"Okay." She gave him the access code to her apartment.

"Thanks. I don't want to miss my date with you tomorrow. Staying the night would save us time."

I know your intention.

She could have called him out and reminded him that their date wouldn't happen until later in the afternoon, but she liked the idea of him staying over. It made her feel safe considering that the Ulkrins were back again.

NINE

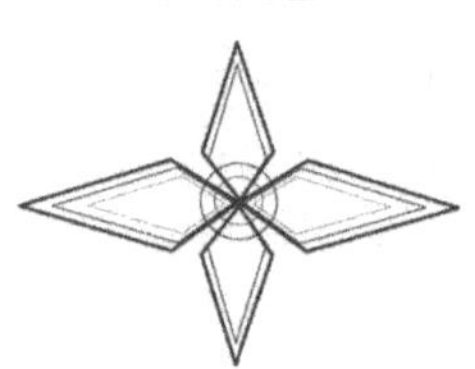

The next morning, Nina washed up and strode out to the living room and found Zeycott snoring on her yellow sofa that was obviously too small for him. She walked over and stared down at the sleeping green man. He had used the small throw blanket, which covered the top half of his body. He wore a tank top with knit pants. One long leg dangled from the sofa edge while the other curled uncomfortably to the side, one bent arm was tucked behind his head while the other hugged a fuzzy accent pillow.

She had gone to bed a little after midnight, but he hadn't returned yet. A smile crept onto his lips, softening the hard planes of his face. Something warmed inside her as she snapped that adorable image of him and tucked it away in her memory.

Nina retrieved a soft blanket from her closet and tossed it over him with caution. He shifted and blinked the sleep from his eyes.

He saw her, smiled, and pulled her down against him. "Morning."

He smelled like her lavender shampoo. "Morning to you." She veered back and sat on the edge of the sofa. "What time did you get back? Why didn't you wake me?"

Zeycott pushed himself up to a sitting position and made room for her beside him. "I didn't want to disturb your peaceful sleep. I took a quick shower and crashed on your couch."

She bumped shoulders with him. "You're such a gentleman for not crawling into bed with me."

He stretched out his legs and slung an arm around her. "You wouldn't think so if you knew what I really wanted to do to you last night. I had these provocative images running through my mind." He took her hand in his. "But I respect you, and I didn't want to take advantage of you. Unless you give me permission to do as I please." His eyes crinkled with mischief. "Do I have your permission for next time?"

Nina retorted, "Do I get your permission to do as *I* desire?"

"Baby, you can do whatever you want, whenever you want. I'll *pay* you."

She let out a loud laugh that echoed through her apartment. She hadn't laughed like that in a long time. Not to mention having a man sleeping on her couch.

Grinning, she poked him in his abdomen. "Then that would make you *my* gigolo."

"I didn't say I'd pay you credits." He leaned in and caught her earlobe with his mouth, nibbling at it. "There are other ways of payment."

Her thighs clenched as his lips wandered down her neck. "Is this how you seduce the females in your life?"

He turned her face to meet his—his expression all serious. "No. You're the only one. I can't stop wanting you."

Zeycott shifted in his seat and grimaced while rubbing his knee.

"Are you okay?" She surveyed him.

"Yeah. I think I slept wrong, and my leg's paying for it now. I'll be fine. How did you sleep?" He rose from the sofa and stretched. "What time do you need to start work? I can work from here today as well."

Satisfied that she saw no more pain on his face, she replied, "I slept well, thanks. I just need to edit some videos, add voiceovers, and complete my outline for the next few months. You can work on the kitchen table or the coffee table." She stacked up the *Galactic LifeStyle* and *Alien Yoga* magazines and moved them to the side table, making room for him.

A tiny spider scurried across the table. "Yuck." Nina assassinated it with one loud smack. She noticed Zeycott eyeing her in disbelief. "I don't like spiders. Now you can have a safe space to work."

"Thank you. I'll inform all arachnids to avoid your home." He smiled. "I'll just situate myself in the kitchen. That way, I won't disrupt you in your corner office. I'll be attending some virtual meetings with my brothers."

She remembered the urgency from last night. "Did you enter the tunnel? Did you encounter any Ulkrins?"

He shook his head. "We didn't see any Ulkrins, but they had been there. The tunnel is a unique portal supported by potent magic. We were in and out quickly. We didn't want to stay long and have them pick up on our energy. We hid some cameras in the tunnel and the surrounding areas."

An icy chill raced down her back, and she shivered. "Something awful is going to happen," Nina said. She could feel it in her bones. She worried for him, his brothers, her sisters, and all the villagers in Saedo.

Zeycott pulled her body toward him. "Don't worry. We have a lot of eyes on the Ulkrins. Saedo isn't the only province trying to obliterate them. We've extracted a map of their land from one of the squirmurs' brains. That will help us destroy them. We don't want any citizen casualties, so we have to be careful with every step we take. Most of all, we don't want anyone to panic." He kissed the top of her head.

"I understand." The nerves in her stomach settled for now. "I'll get breakfast ready while you wash up. Then we can start our workday."

Nina and Zeycott jumped into work like a couple who had been living together for years. Everything flowed effortlessly, as though they knew what each needed and wanted. When he went to grab a bottle of blue water, he got her one as well. When she craved a snack, she dropped a bag of pink chips on his table.

Nina concentrated on her videos, while Zeycott discussed strategies with his brothers. She wasn't sure if she was supposed to be listening to their conversation about the Ulkrins. If Zeycott didn't want her to hear anything, he would have put on his headphones. He trusted her, and her heart felt full with this knowledge.

She glued her ears to their serious discussion about the Ulkrins. Concern for him twisted in her gut. Zeycott and his brothers—some of whom were her sisters' lovers—were in the front line of danger. She absorbed everything they said. She even looked at the map of Agarrek when Zeycott expanded it into the air. It showed that the Province of Agarrek had been flourishing before the Ulkrins—who were a rebellious faction —took over. Apparently, the native star-beings of Agarrek were gentle and didn't have the army to fight off the rebellion.

Knowing these details made her hate the Ulkrins even more. In the beginning, she had thought Agarrek was *their* province, a dark settlement full of evil aliens. But they had just taken over the land and ruled it as their own.

She didn't even realize she had clenched her fists until Zeycott said, "You look angry. Do you need to take a break for a special Zeycott yoga session to release some tension? It'll be 'yogasmic.'"

Oh. My. God. She didn't realize he could be this creative.

He yanked her from despair and made her smile with a unique word. Her shoulders shook with laughter. "Shouldn't you be concentrating on work?"

"I was until I saw your clenched fists and thought you might need help unclenching them. I know someone who's desperate to have those hands on him."

Her eyes lowered to the prominent rod tenting his knit pants.

"You're supposed to be working. How can you be aroused while chatting with your brothers about evil aliens?"

"That was *minutes* ago. All I have to do is look at you and I'm hot and bothered. It's not my fault."

"*You.*" She pointed to Zeycott. "Get back to work. And *you.*" She pointed to his erection. "Behave." She swung her chair back to face her two screens and tried *very* hard to concentrate on work.

Zeycott laughed. "I guess it worked. Your hands are relaxed now."

Nina didn't turn around. If she did, she might jump his bones. And neither of them would get anything done.

After a break for lunch, the hours flew by, and it was time for the flying yoga class.

TEN

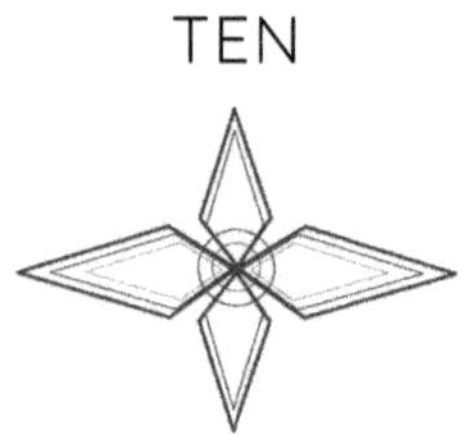

As expected, all eyes followed Zeycott when they walked into class. He wore a fitted dark top and matching loose pants, and she wore some of Inga's yoga wear that was like a second skin. She stole a glance at him. He didn't seem to mind that he was the only male taking that class.

Some of the female star-beings had exceptional figures. For a moment, Nina glanced down at her petite body and couldn't help the tiny sliver of insecurity crawling up her back. But Zeycott didn't even glance at them.

He held her hand as they walked over to an area by the wall.

"Are you doing okay?" she whispered.

"Why wouldn't I be?"

"Because you're the only male here."

He shrugged. "I don't care. They can look all they want. I'm here to make a fool out of myself for *you*, hoping I'll get rewarded tonight."

His eyes pierced hers, and heat zipped through her. "Class is starting. Pay attention."

She stepped into a circle drawn on the floor that marked everyone's position. The markings allowed for enough space between each student. That answered her question of why the room was so big and there were only twelve students in the class.

"Welcome, everyone. My name is Marcelle, and I'll be your instructor today," said the bright green female star-being with short purple hair. She had a body made to seduce and a tail that added to her allure. Her fingers pointed toward the ceiling. "Energy streams will descend from above. They're programmed to assist you in the first twenty minutes. After that, a screen will pop up and you can choose the next level. For beginners, I suggest choosing anything on level one. We'll warm up first with some basic stretching. Just follow my moves."

Nina glanced over at Zeycott, who winked at her.

After the warmup, a robotic disc flew over and hovered above her head. It sent out streams of energies that flowed around her like colorful ribbons. Copying Marcelle, Nina reached for one stream and was surprised when she could grasp it. The energy streams lifted Nina above the ground.

"Don't forget to breathe and tighten those core muscles!" Marcelle's voice boomed through the speakers.

Using her arm muscles, Nina held tight to the energy stream and performed a few flips, while keeping her legs straight as if she were a gymnast. She looked over at Zeycott, who could follow the steps with ease.

Nina accomplished the warrior pose, the triangle pose, the reverse bicycle pose, and even the crane pose, which was one of the most advanced poses. But to do these in the air, with energy ribbons, took yoga to a whole new level.

Her breathing was deeper, so her body inhaled more oxygen. She flipped and twisted into the scorpion pose, untwisted herself back to plank before resuming into the boat pose. With help from the virtual screen that followed her around, she adjusted herself when her body misaligned. She even tried swimming in the air, which made her feel like she was flying. For those with height phobias, this class would have been scary, even though there were energy ribbons keeping them safe.

From the twenty minutes of "practice," Nina worked her whole body. Flying yoga was no joke. When she descended to the ground, it took her a moment to find her equilibrium. The five-minute break allowed her to check up on Zeycott.

"What do you think?" She handed him a bottle of blue water and sipped from her own.

"Fantastic. I didn't know I could flip and do all of those weird poses. The energetic beams really helped, though." He flicked her an amused look. "I saw you in the scorpion and crow poses. They're sexy." He tapped his head. "They're etched in my brain now. I want to see you perform that for me when we get home."

"Then I get to see you in a pose of my choice."

"Fine. I've got plenty of practice now."

When class resumed, Nina and Zeycott looked at the options on the beginner's level. She reviewed the classes in which they could work with a partner.

"There's such a thing as a 'lover's tangle?' Let's try it." Zeycott pointed to the third one down the list.

That sounded interesting.

The lover's tangle consisted of poses that placed them close together. The energetic streams helped them get into positions that would have been impossible on the ground. Their arms and legs tangled, almost like an intimate dance in the air.

With their faces close to each other, Zeycott stole a kiss before the energetic streams whisked him away. In a superman pose that tightened her arms, abs, and legs, she flew over to him, around him, and squeezed his butt. She didn't care if anyone watched their playful yoga session.

The lover's tangle was an interesting yoga concept she hadn't considered. To her, yoga had always been about anchoring the body, mind, and soul. The lover's tangle was the practice that enhanced sexual energy—the creative life force in all beings. When life force was in abundance, the body, mind, and spirit thrived. An idea sparked in her mind, but she'd let it sit and marinate before deciding if she wanted to do something about it.

When the session ended, her body felt nimble. She toweled off her face and gulped down an entire bottle of blue water. She offered him a towel for his sweaty face and hair.

"I need a shower." She shoved the dirty towels into the duffle bag that Zeycott carried.

His eyes gleamed. "Me too. We can save time and shower together."

She liked that idea, but she'd let him wonder. "We'll see."

They exited the class and headed toward his rider. As Zeycott tossed the duffle back into his trunk, a scream erupted in the parking lot. "Help me!"

Like a trained soldier, his gaze whipped toward the direction of the cry. Then he rushed over to Nina. "Get in the rider and stay there. I need to check this out."

She was about to protest when a female star-being ran

past, an Ulkrin beast chasing after her. Nina had seen images of its kind on the news, but in real life, it appeared larger and more frightening. The creature looked like a cross between a wolf and bear. It snarled, and rows of sharp teeth glinted from the lampposts in the lot. The beast had bulging red eyes and a long, spiky tail.

"Get in, Nina. Call for backup." Zeycott ushered her into his rider and shut the door.

She didn't want to separate from him, but fear clenched her stomach. Zeycott reached for his blaster, which was hidden on the side of his door. He slammed the driver's side door shut and rushed after the Ulkrin beast. He aimed and shot at it. It hit a hind leg, and the beast roared in pain. Another shriek escaped its mouth as though calling for help.

Frozen with fear, Nina didn't know what to do. Unlike Vanessa, who knew how to use a gun, Nina was clueless about self-defense. She called the emergency alert and described the situation. She voiced a message to her sisters to inform them to go home in case they were out.

Five more Ulkrin beasts with long snouts ran up near Zeycott's rider and sniffed the air. They looked like mutant bears and wolves, with a mixture of features she couldn't identify. But these creatures had two mouths and possessed spikes along their backs, not to mention they were twice the size of the first creature.

Students from the yoga session screamed and ran back inside the studio. Shoppers from the plaza hid in their riders, autobuses—anything that kept them out of view. Nina didn't know where the frightened star-being had run off to. Hopefully, she found a safe place to hide. Zeycott sent another blast into the wounded Ulkrin beast, and it collapsed.

A massive Ulkrin beast surfaced from somewhere in the lot and leaped over to the dead beast.

It snarled. "I will kill you for hurting my babies."

Shit, it talks! Nina recalled her siblings mentioning something about the mother beast being more evolved. The rest of the pack rushed over to the mother beast.

Terror gripped Nina at the danger looming around them. Zeycott was only one soldier. There was no way he'd defeat all these creatures without getting injured. Where were the other soldiers? Why hadn't they come yet?

A stream of cold sweat trickled down her back as she tried to think of how she could help Zeycott.

Frantic, she searched his rider for a weapon and found a metal stick about a foot long lying on the back seat. It had a button on the handle. Nina grabbed it and hopped out of the rider. Two Ulkrin beasts turned their attention to her. Terror trembled through her, making her lightheaded. She inhaled several breaths to calm her body. She gripped the metal stick tighter and pressed the button. A beam of electricity hissed from the tip and fanned out into a series of lightning bolts.

From his stance, Zeycott met her eyes, and fear splashed on his face. She couldn't let him fight these awful creatures while she sat in his rider and watched. He'd saved her once, the least she could do was help now. And if she died today, it was worth it. The past few weeks had been the happiest moments of her life.

Think positive, Nina.

She shook off the despair and looked the Ulkrin beasts in the eyes. One jumped at her, and she screamed and whacked the metal stick against its body. Energy zapped and singed its skin. The smell of burned fur and flesh filled the air, making her gag.

Nina stumbled back and lost her balance, and pain bloomed on her body. The wounded beast shrieked as it struggled to charge at her again. There was no skill to what she was doing. She was merely acting on instincts. This was her first time hurting a living thing that wasn't a nasty insect or spider. She should feel bad about it, but she didn't feel any remorse at the moment. If she didn't kill the creature, it would definitely kill her. Zeycott appeared by her side and helped her up from the ground. She didn't even remember falling on her ass.

"You okay?" He flared his nostrils. "I told you to stay in the rider."

She didn't like his tone and answered with the same, "And I don't want to watch you die."

She looked past his shoulders, stepped forward, and stabbed at an Ulkrin beast that pounced at his back. The metal stick scorched its paw. It retreated and growled at her.

"See? There are too many of these things. You need my help."

A small smile crept onto his lips. "Press the button two more times for maximum power. Hold the taser like this." He showed her the right way to use his weapon, which didn't require whacking or anything. The power of the electrical current extended far enough, and she was ready to kill any creature coming at her.

Nina didn't know where this courage stemmed from. She should have been paralyzed with fear, but when she saw the pack of Ulkrin beasts wanting to devour Zeycott, something snapped in her. All she could feel was this powerful need to keep him safe. She wasn't a soldier. She was just a woman . . . trying to understand her heart. Yes, that was it.

Sirens blasted in the air, and the emergency autobuses arrived. Soldiers poured out, and relief settled when she spotted Raeko, Maeson, Osayik, Arkon, Jarzell, and their other brothers. They fought the beasts, but the mother beast rushed Zeycott and Nina.

Zeycott blasted the beast several times. Blood gushed from her neck, body, and legs, but she didn't collapse like her offspring. Her tail thrashed as she eyed Nina. Nina held the taser rod at the ready.

The mother beast pounced and reached for Nina with her bloody claws. Nina shot out a bolt of electricity, blasting her square in the face. She snarled and retreated as her red eyes flared in defiance. The mother beast wasn't going down easy. She roared in anger and thrashed her tail wildly.

Zeycott blasted more beams into her. "Flekken die!"

With the blasts entering her body and blood pouring from her, the mother beast still didn't give up. She growled and charged at Nina again, and Nina didn't have time to defend herself. Zeycott threw himself between Nina and the mother beast, all while sending a series of blasts into her head. The beast thudded to the ground, and something cracked.

Zeycott collapsed, and her heart stopped at the way his leg bent abnormally. A blue bone pierced through his green flesh, and his face distorted in agony. "Ugh! *Flekken!*"

"Oh my God!" Nina dropped beside him. "Your knee!"

Tears blurred her eyes, and she wiped them away so she could see him better. She'd never seen bones sticking out from flesh like this. She wanted to help him, touch him, soothe him—anything to relieve his misery. But she didn't know what to do.

She shouted to his brothers for help. "Over here! He needs help!"

"I'm okay," Zeycott told her, even when the color on his face dulled and his eyes drooped.

"You're not okay," Nina cried, holding his body against hers.

Please don't die. He'd been injured because of her. He'd saved her life *again.*

"Nina . . . don't cry," he whispered and passed out.

She bit her bottom lip so hard it bled. The pain helped keep her from thinking of the inevitable.

She held his unconscious body and clasped his hand in hers. "Please don't die."

Raeko and Jarzell rushed over with a robotic cot. "We've got him." She watched the powerful soldiers assist her lover on the cot.

"Is he . . ." She couldn't form the words.

"He's not dead." Raeko placed a hand on her shoulder while Jarzell escorted the robotic cot into the autobus. "We're taking him to Grandma Ova."

"Why not take him to the hospital?" Nina asked.

"The physicians at the hospital won't be able to help. Grandma Ova knows about his unique condition."

This must be what he's been keeping from me.

"I'm coming with you," Nina said. "Please."

"Okay, but let the emergency crew examine you first. It'll save Grandma Ova time. I want her to focus on Zeycott."

Nina nodded and followed Raeko toward the emergency crew at the autobus. "The mother beast broke his bones."

"His bones are getting more fragile these days. I didn't realize they had turned blue." Raeko gestured to the autobus with crew members waiting to assist her.

"What do you mean? Your bones aren't blue?"

"No, they're the same color as yours."

Nina's mouth dropped open at the image of Zeycott's blue bone piercing through his knee. She had too many questions, but they could wait. The only thing she cared about now was Zeycott's safety. Would he recover without problems?

While the emergency crew examined her, she replayed the day in her mind. It had been a wonderful day until this . . .

She glanced up at the starry sky. *You heard my wish, didn't you? You delivered him to me. Please don't take him away.*

Hot tears slid down her cheeks.

"Am I hurting you?" asked the bald medic.

She shook her head. "No, I'm fine."

He continued cleansing and disinfecting the scratches on her wrists and forearm and treated them with an antibiotic sealant. "You're all set." She didn't even recall how she got them. The adrenaline rush had numbed her from everything.

"Thank you." She wiped the tears from her eyes and prepared for a soldier to drop her off at Grandma Ova's house.

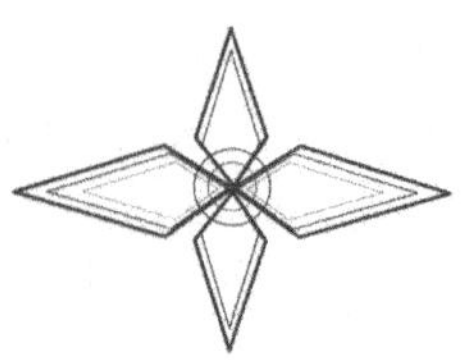

ELEVEN

By the time Nina arrived, Grandma Ova had already situated Zeycott in a quiet room on a bed. He lay unconscious with his injured leg suspended about a foot above the bed by beams of energy, similar to the ones used at the flying yoga studio. The only difference was that these energy beams moved like vines.

"What are they?" Nina pointed to the vine that sprouted a new leaf. The energetic vines weren't connected to a larger plant. They didn't come from the wall, the bed, or the floor.

"A Zintakan vine gifted to me by a good friend. She's a healer from a different planet."

Satisfied with the answer, Nina turned her attention to his knee, which had been cleansed and bandaged with gauze. She didn't see any bloodstains.

A headache throbbed at her temples. "How are his bones? Is he going to be okay? Is he still in pain?"

"He's stable right now. Let's go into the kitchen. I'll make you some tea for the headache, and then we can talk."

Nina dropped into a cushioned chair. Grandma Ova's

kitchen was three times the size of Nina's. The woman could probably feed all of Saedo if she wanted to. Nina had never dreamed of such an extensive kitchen. She didn't mind cooking, but she minded cleaning. If Lorinz had to clean a kitchen that size, in addition to helping her with other chores, she'd have to buy extra charging crystals to keep him operational.

"Here. Drink this." Grandma Ova set down a white mug with bright green liquids. A flower floated at the top, sending out white wisps. "It'll soothe your nerves and take care of that pounding headache."

"Thank you." Nina sipped and inhaled the sweet scent of the flower. Like magic, her headache diminished. "Wow . . . My headache's gone. That was fast."

Grandma Ova smiled. "Your headache was caused by stress. This stress-relieving flower has a sweet aroma that targets the neurons in your brain. Scent is a powerful medicine."

The wonders of this planet continued to astound her.

Nina placed the cup down and studied Grandma Ova. She had white hair in a classic bob cut, hugging her face beautifully. Her green skin, amber eyes, and warm smile made Nina feel at home. She wore a soft yellow top with wide pants that had large pockets. Looking at her made Nina miss her parents, who died in a car crash a long time ago. Emma had been the older sister who had taken care of the six siblings.

"I like your haircut," Nina said. She couldn't pull off that short style.

Grandma Ova touched her white hair. "Oh, thank you. Sasha swung by the other day to give me a trim."

Her sister had made a name for herself at the Hair Spectrum, but she took on personal clients at their home. Nina was due for a haircut soon.

Nina wrapped her fingers around the cup and let out a heavy sigh. "Will Zeycott be able to walk again?" A sliver of orange mist snaked around her wrists with silver sparkles. She waved her fingers through the mist and dispersed the sparks.

"I hope so." Grandma Ova sipped from her cup.

That wasn't the answer Nina wanted to hear.

"Do you see his mist color?" Grandma Ova asked, her amber eyes curious.

That caught Nina off guard. "I see an orange mist with silver sparks, but I'm not sure if it's his. I know about the mist. I hadn't shared it with anyone in case the orange mist was something else. Or it belongs to another star-being."

She didn't want it to be anyone's but Zeycott's. It scared her to find out the truth.

"You can ask him when he wakes. He can tell you his mist color."

Nina drummed her fingers on the rim of her cup and stared into the drink. "The first time I saw it, he wasn't even around."

"The mist can linger long after the individual is gone. Did you see him that day?"

Nina recalled the pain on his face. "Oh, yes. He and his brothers were at the marketplace. But then they all left, and I browsed an art gallery. I saw some of Rita's paintings and other artists' sculptures. There was even a fossil of some animal with odd carvings on its bones."

Grandma Ova smiled and placed her cup down. "The mist definitely belongs to Zeycott. He donated a part of his bone to an experiment that extended a cat's life. The animal had air pockets in its bones, like Zeycott. But it eventually died from corra failure. That fossil had Zeycott's energies. It was a cutting-edge experiment that the province loves to display."

The story settled the queasiness in her stomach. "What exactly is wrong with his bones?"

Grandma Ova pulled up a virtual screen from the table. "I've been working with a physician down at the hospital regarding Zeycott. My herbal medicine has been helping him to maintain his health. Look at this diagram."

Nina had never been interested in human biology or anatomy, but now she was curious about alien bone structure.

"The bone is composed of several layers. This section is spongy bone. But look closely at the pattern of his porous bone and the honeycombed appearance."

Nina studied the "air pockets" made from various shapes, like circles, triangles, squares, pentagons, and hexagons. Was it even possible to have so many shapes?

The more she stared at it, the more it tickled her memory. She had seen these shapes somewhere. An image popped into her mind. "I remember now. I carved a sculpture of him. Somehow, I created these geometric designs on the side of his face. I didn't know I had done it. It felt like a trance."

"Maybe it was. Your energies resonate with each other, so maybe you stepped into a trance where your corra carved what was in it." Grandma Ova's wise eyes crinkled.

Could her heart energy guide her hands to create? She had no words, but it made sense in a bizarre way.

She turned her attention back to Zeycott. "What do all the geometric shapes mean?"

"Zeycott believes he's sick, but I think he's blessed with a gift I'm still trying to uncover. Most star-beings have one or two geometric air pockets, but he's different. His mother had the same illness, but she had another disease that destroyed her body quickly. So I understand why he feels hopeless."

"If he hadn't used his body to block me from the Ulkrin beast, his knee wouldn't have been injured."

"What happened wasn't your fault. Those beasts are massive. Zeycott's bone density is actually improving from when I last saw him. It has also turned blue. That's unheard of. Something else is going on here, but I need time to experiment." Grandma Ova swiped off the screen. "Don't worry, Nina. He'll be all right. That's my gut feeling."

Guilt surfaced and tightened her tummy. If she had stayed in the rider as he had asked, he wouldn't have needed to use his body to shield her.

Grandma Ova's eyes softened. "There's a special bond between the two of you."

"What do you mean?"

"When I was treating his knee, something extraordinary occurred. He kept calling your name while he was unconscious. Each time he called for you, his bone sparked."

"What?" Nina had never heard of such a thing.

"Not only that, as I was trying to fuse his bones together with an energy band to promote new bone growth, I noticed that his bone had already regenerated itself. I know he'll be okay. But we need to understand why it's happening and what will come of it."

Nina bit her bottom lip, trying to envision what Grandma Ova just described. "I'm speechless."

"It's a unique phenomenon." Grandma Ova tapped her fingers. "I read about it once in the Silver Text."

Nina remembered that Rita and Jarzell had found the Copper Text not too long ago. Those sacred books held divine knowledge that helped Saedo thrive.

Nina made the connection. "What color did his bone spark?"

"Silver."

"His orange mist has silver sparks too. Even his eyes spark when he looks at me."

The grin on Grandma Ova's face stretched into a wide smile. "That's because he's attracted to you. He's got all the qualities a woman wants. A handsome face, a wonderful corra, and a body that's built like a machine. That means power and stamina, know what I mean?" She wiggled her eyebrows.

Oh, God. Laughing, Nina covered her face with her hands. She didn't want to give out intimate details. It was too embarrassing, like talking to your mother or grandmother about sex.

"We haven't gotten that far yet. But I'll be happy to report back if you'd like."

Grandma Ova grinned and waved a hand. "Oh, that's okay. I know exactly what happens behind closed doors. He'll satisfy you; I can tell you that. I had my share of sexual adventures when I was young. I was wild and explorative, and I can see that adventurous gleam in your eyes. Have fun with each other. Life can be unpredictable."

Nina could imagine Grandma Ova catching the eyes of males everywhere. Even at her age of one thousand and three hundred solar cycles, she looked like someone in her sixties.

Her face still had the fine bone structure and grace that came with aging well. The high vibration in Saedo definitely helped with the longevity of these star-beings.

Nina had a sexual adventure planned for Zeycott prior to this horrific event. She'd postpone it until he was well again. His bone abnormality fascinated her. What was happening to him? Despite what Grandma Ova said about the bone regeneration, Nina couldn't help but worry. Right now, everything was just speculation. Grandma Ova still needed to experiment to find concrete answers.

What if she discovered something dire? What if . . .

She stopped her mind from wandering into dark territory. Instead, she concentrated on what *could* help him.

"Do you think his condition is linked to the Silver Text?" A warmth brushed along her cheek. "Maybe there's something in the text that could heal him. Or shed some light on his situation."

"My thoughts are aligned with yours. This spark from his bone is new. I think that's a sign we have to pay attention to. Ever since you and your sisters arrived in Saedo, the energy fields have changed for the better. There's a potent vibration of love that's taken over Saedo, which is beautiful and necessary. With the rise of darkness, we need more love to battle it."

Nina gasped. "I almost forgot. I saw the orange mist form a female face that fluctuated between an animal and a star-being. I saw it twice. It just looked at me for a while and disappeared."

"One of Saedo's ancestors has contacted you. They're keeping the sacred texts hidden until the right individuals can find them. Your encounter means that they've chosen you for the task."

"Where are the texts? How do I even know where to begin?"

"They're placed strategically in areas that would connect to you." Grandma Ova placed a hand over Nina's. "My advice is to open yourself to the ancestors. Entertain the idea that you could talk to them. Once they sense the barriers are down, they'll be more accessible. Rita could speak to them."

Before living in Saedo, Nina couldn't have fathomed speaking to a supernatural being, but now that she was communicating with star-beings and other strange creatures, the idea of talking to a spirit wasn't that farfetched.

"I could do that." Nina yawned and glanced at the clock on Grandma Ova's wall. It was midnight, and she needed a hot shower and a change of clothing.

Grandma Ova gathered the cups and placed them in the sink.

"You wouldn't have any spare clothing I can borrow for tonight, would you? I'd like to stay and monitor him."

"I have plenty of clothes available for my visitors. I'll also get fresh towels for you." She strode down the hall to a closet. "You can stay in the guest room across from Zeycott's. He should sleep through the night. I gave him a strong sleep serum and an extra dose of painkillers. I can't have him moving around while the bone-mending gauze is inducing new bone growth."

Knowing that Zeycott was well taken care of, Nina mentally released the anxiety from her mind and her body. The much-needed hot shower pounded her tense muscles and soothed any residual stress that had carried over from the event. She slipped into a soft pajama set that could also be worn as casual clothing and checked on Zeycott.

The energy bands had lowered his leg to suspend about five inches above the bed rather than the whole foot. An image of his deformed leg surfaced in her mind, and she shook it away. He must have experienced excruciating pain. She stared at the injury, which hadn't changed from when she saw it earlier. No blood oozed through the gauze.

He looked peaceful, sleeping with a slight snore. She kissed his cheek and returned to her guest room across the hall as fatigue dragged her into bed. She was about to turn off the light on the nightstand when the orange mist appeared and flowed in front of her. The mist formed a vaguely female face. Silver sparks glittered around her hair.

Trust your instincts.

The lovely voice popped into her head. Grandma Ova had told her to entertain speaking to the ancestor of the land.

Nina didn't sense any fear from this stranger. "Do you need my help? What can I do to assist Zeycott?"

The mist dispersed into ribbons that slithered around the room. *"My son needs you. You'll know how to help him."*

Nina's heart raced. "You're his mother?"

The mist combined to form the face again. Two large silver sparks flickered like eyes. The face didn't move as it spoke to her mind.

"Yes. I'm Surell. Thank you for helping him. You've expanded his corra in a way no one else has. That's powerful. You're healing him in unimaginable ways."

"But he got hurt today . . . because of me."

"You're his forever mate, and he'd give his life for you." The face moved closer.

Reflex had her veering back a bit. "You've been watching over him?"

"All parents watch over their children."

Nina thought about her parents, and she knew they were doing their best to keep an eye on their seven daughters.

"I'm in a place between the seen and unseen worlds. Right now, I'm edgewalking to connect with you. Know that the sparks from his bones are because of you. Your energy is boosting his healing. He needs it. The sparks are breaking up the rare disease. He has osteomites. It's very difficult to heal because the bug shapeshifts. That is the key here, its power. Relay this message to Grandma Ova."

"You can't communicate with her?"

She shook her head and orange wisps waved around her face. *"Your energy allows me to edgewalk. It doesn't work with her. I've tried."*

Was the disease similar to a flu virus that shifts? There was really no "cure" for it because there were so many mutations of it. If Zeycott's illness continuously mutated, how could they ever heal him completely?

Concern pricked at her. "I want to help him, but I'm not sure how."

"Every time he sees you, his bone marrow reacts to you. His bones shift and heal themselves. Your love has given him a chance to survive. He thinks he's dying because, when the bone sparks, pain escalates in him. He believes his bones are breaking bit by bit, and they had been until you came along. Now the pain is sharper, but that's because the healing is more powerful."

It sounded like a paradox. How could the pain be worse when his body was healing? She couldn't dissect the intricate web of miracles. She would just accept that something magical was happening to Zeycott.

Now she understood the pain she'd seen on his face. He believed that being with her was the reason for his pain—the reason for his demise. Was this why he hadn't made a move until now?

She remembered his words during their intimate moment. *Nina, you're killing me. But I don't give a shit.*

"I assume you can't connect to Zeycott?"

"That would have been too easy. The Cosmos usually has a lesson and makes things more interesting."

"I'll share what you've told me with him," Nina said. "He'd be shocked that I spoke to you."

The misty face smiled. *"He sees me in his dreams."*

Nina asked a tough question she couldn't ignore. "Is there any way to obliterate this disease?"

"Find the Silver Text. Ancient knowledge is in there."

"Do you know where the tablet is? Can you tell me?"

The Silver Text was one of the three Sacred Tablets. The Copper Text had been found and returned to the Saedo government for safekeeping. She wasn't sure about the Gold Text. Now it was her turn to search for the Silver Text.

"I can't. That would go against the cosmic law. If I do that, the Scared Tablet will lose its power, its magic. This is your journey with Zeycott. Find it together. Trust your instincts."

Her face faded with the orange mists. When the last few sparkles disappeared, Nina replayed the unbelievable experience in her head. There was hope for Zeycott, and that motivated her.

She needed to get some sleep so she could share this information with Grandma Ova and Zeycott tomorrow.

TWELVE

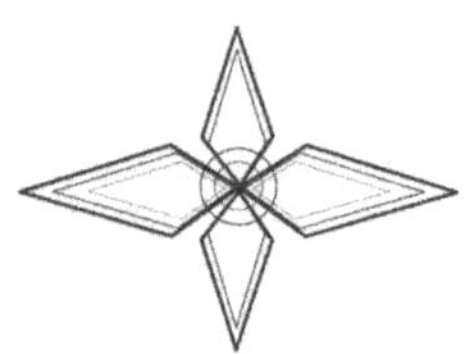

Nina inspected Zeycott as he walked over to the table for breakfast with a metal cane. She had expected him to have a crutch or even use the fancy wheelchair that Grandma had available.

"Are you sure you're supposed to be walking around like this? Shouldn't you be sitting in one place, so you don't accidentally dislocate something you're not supposed to? What if you injure yourself again? Are you in pain? I can get your breakfast for you. Be careful there! That stool could have tripped you!" She rushed over and grabbed his arm, even though he didn't seem to need her assistance.

A smirk formed on his face. "I'm fine."

"You have a *cane*, you're not fine." She bent down, furrowed her eyebrows, and stared at the fresh gauze that glowed around his knee. She could see his green skin and a subtle scar.

"Are you done?" He tapped her shoulder. She glanced up and met his beaming gaze. "I love that you're concerned about me. It makes this all worth it."

"Don't say such things." She clamped a hand over his mouth. "I only want to hear positive words coming from you, okay? Don't give negativity any power. I don't want to see you that way again. It terrified me."

His smile faded, and he gripped her hand, kissing it. "I'm feeling wonderful. Really. I don't know what Grandma Ova did, but I can hardly feel any pain. The energy bond-mending gauze is keeping my muscles warm and bone intact."

When Grandma Ova walked over to the table with a tray of goodies, Nina asked, "Should he be walking around? It hasn't even been twenty-four hours since the injury. Bones can't heal that fast."

"You're right. Normal bones can't, but his are *abnormal*." Using wooden tongs, Grandma Ova placed a fruit tart on a small white dish. "Do you want some coffee to go with this pastry?"

Nina hadn't even told them about her experience from last night. "Yes, I'd love some, thanks." She assisted Zeycott into the chair beside her and got him a fruit tart too.

Grandma Ova flicked an amused glance at Zeycott. "You're getting too pampered."

"Don't get used to it," Nina teased as she sat down and grabbed her mug of coffee. She sipped, sighed, and sipped again. Later, she would ask about the coffee. She turned to Zeycott. "I met your mother last night."

He spat out coffee. "You dreamed about her?"

"No." Nina looked over at Grandma Ova. "She was 'edgewalking' to communicate with me. I'm not sure what that is, but I assumed it's something that has to do with two worlds."

Grandma Ova's eyes brightened. "You're right. Edge-walking is when someone is walking on the 'edge' that connects various dimensions. That space when one world overlaps the other is divine. It's quantum, meaning you can't really locate it. The cosmic map is multidimensional. There are no longitude or latitude lines to guide you."

Nina tried to wrap that idea in her mind. It was difficult, and yet, somehow, it all made sense. She didn't need to know *exactly* how it worked. The fact that she had experienced it made it believable.

Zeycott's eyes focused intently on hers. "What did she say to you?"

"That your bones resonate with my energy. The 'spark' from your bones is because your bones are shifting and healing." She licked her dry lips. "I'm not sure how, but my energy is helping you heal. The pain that you feel is not because of your bones weakening, Zeycott. It's because they're mending."

A quizzical eyebrow rose above his right eye. "She told you all of that?"

"She wanted to contact you and Grandma Ova to relay the message, but she couldn't connect to any of you. I'm the reason your bones are blue. Somehow, my energy inspired your bone to change color."

To say that out loud sounded bizarre, but it was the truth. Nothing should surprise her anymore, and yet, the stuff that came from her mouth baffled her.

"You're the link to Zeycott's healing," Grandma Ova said. "Did she say anything about his condition? I've always wondered what she knew about her osteomites. It would help me and the doctors heal him better if we had her feedback."

"She wanted you to know that the virus, or whatever causes the osteomites, can shapeshift."

"What?" Zeycott blurted out.

"I had the same reaction. It seems like the bug is intelligent."

Grandma Ova slapped a hand on the table, her eyes gleaming with hope. "This is excellent information, Nina. I'll need to find something that can also shapeshift to counteract it. Let me explain. The body has a powerful immune system that knows how to fight off foreign objects. This is the same for humans, aliens, angels, any beings." Her hand gestured to herself then to Nina. "Though each race offers a slightly different version, the approach is the same. Your body attacks anything that wants to harm you. I need to find something that corresponds to this bug, which is a mite or virus. Osteomites are rare, and they've perplexed me and scientists in this province. We couldn't save Zeycott's mom because we didn't have any information about the damn mites. It's a mutation from harmless blood mites, which are necessary for bone marrow growth."

Nina's body shivered as she imagined what these mites looked like and decided she didn't want to know. Bugs, especially spiders, weren't her thing.

"Your mom said that there's a remedy in the Silver Text that could help. We have to find it."

"That's fantastic news." Grandma Ova patted Zeycott's arm. "That's why she contacted you, Nina."

A sadness washed over Zeycott's face. "I always wondered if she had felt pain when she passed."

"I think whatever pain she went through has been replaced by love for her son," Grandma Ova said.

Zeycott offered a warm smile. "How can she be sure that the Silver Text will have a cure?"

Nina understood his uncertainty. His mom had died from this disease that had also affected his life. To hear about a potential cure gave him hope—hope that would devastate him if it didn't come true. He was teetering on the edge of belief and disbelief.

Nina didn't know how she understood all of that, but she did. When she started anew in Saedo, she also wavered between hope and loss. But she chose hope.

"You're a wonderful son, Zeycott," Grandma Ova said, "and Surell knows that. I know that too, which is why I requested to treat you personally. Do you think I offer this special treatment to everyone?"

"Yes." He smiled. "You're Saedo's grandmother. You care for everyone."

She laughed. "I wish I could care for everyone, but I'm just one person. I have to replenish my energy too. I do what I can, but I wanted to help *you*. Your energy is needed for Saedo to thrive. Let's just say that I had a feeling you would play a role in Saedo's evolution." Her gaze swerved over to Nina. "And I know you and your sisters are needed here too. Each of you brings a unique vibration that allows for more magic to occur."

"I don't know where the Silver Text is, though. Surell couldn't tell me."

"She can't break the cosmic law. Things are already in motion. You need to find it. All I can tell you is that it's in a tattoo parlor or a museum." Grandma Ova had seen all the Sacred Tablets. She had a unique connection to them.

"How do you know this? When did they go missing?" Nina asked. She didn't recall seeing anything on the news.

"I'm part of the Ancestral Council, which works with other realms. I can connect to certain ancestors. There's no need for everyone to know about me and the council because things like that are too complicated to explain. I want to keep things simple for the villagers. Certain things are safer when they're not broadcasted, you know?" She looked at Nina and Zeycott, and they nodded in agreement.

That explained a lot of things about the wise woman. Nina could only imagine the powerful will and patience required to hold so much wisdom and to only give out enough when the time was right. Her brain wasn't wired for something so complex.

Grandma Ova continued, "The Silver Text isn't missing —it is hidden, by choice. Its disappearance is all part of a plan. I'll help you as much as I can. Even though I'm part of the council, I don't know everything. No one knows everything."

"I've never seen the tablet before. How do I know what I'm looking for?" Nina turned to Zeycott. "Have you seen it?"

Zeycott shook his head. "But I have an image of the Copper Text." He pulled up a virtual screen, logged into the government site, and showed them a few images.

"They all look similar with a rectangular shape," Grandma Ova said. "The tablets are made from the brown Saedonite crystal. This rare stone went through an alchemical process that made it look like glass. But it's a natural stone, not engineered by star-beings or any machines."

"The Copper Text was discovered inside Rita's sketchbook, so the Silver Text has to be in a place that connects to us." Hope illumed like a lightbulb as Nina sent Zeycott a stunned look. "Do you think it's at Versatile Ink?"

"I have some books and tablets on my bookcase, but I don't remember seeing anything out of the ordinary."

"We should look." Nina glanced over at Grandma Ova, who wore a contemplative expression. "What's on your mind?"

"The Silver Text is different from the Copper Text," she said. "Each tablet carries a different mission. The Silver Text has a different lesson."

An uncomfortable feeling settled in Nina's stomach. "What's different about it?"

"There's a sacrifice that needs to happen. I don't know exactly what that means. I just know that the 'sacrifice' is a word associated with this tablet. I don't want to give you the wrong impression that it's a bad thing. I just want you to know what you're getting yourself into. Just keep that in mind."

Of course there's a catch. Nothing worthwhile was ever easy. She didn't want to discourage Zeycott, who needed healing and hope right now.

Nina narrowed her eyes and pursed her lips. "Maybe it means we have to *sacrifice* the dead body of an Ulkrin beast."

Grandma Ova laughed. "I like the way she thinks. She is perfect for you."

Zeycott offered her a small smile. "She is."

Orange mist emerged from the exposed skin on his face and neck, moving toward her. Silver sparks glittered within the misty ribbons. This was her first time seeing the orange mist seep through his skin like steam from a hot shower.

Zeycott waved his fingers through the orange mist that gathered around him.

"Wow." Nina played with the mist dancing in front of her.

"You see my mist?"

She met his eyes. "It's a beautiful orange with silver sparks, right?"

The sadness that had been in his eyes vanished. "Tell me when you first saw it."

"It's a beautiful night for a walk in the pink grass field," Grandma Ova said. "Why don't you take a walk and discuss the mist?"

"That's a great idea," Nina said.

Grandma Ova got up from her seat. "I know you're both eager to find the Sacred Tablet. But Zeycott needs to heal before you start searching. There is a rush, and there is no rush. You take care of what's important first, do all that you can do this day, and everything else will fall into place." She jerked her chin toward the window. "The sweet aroma is good for the both of you. Breathe and live. The rest will come when it comes. You can't stop the suns from shining. You can't stop the wind from blowing. In other words, you can't stop what's meant to happen."

Nina would've loved to spend more time listening to Grandma Ova elaborate on her riddles. Her sisters had mentioned that Grandma Ova spoke about things that had an undercurrent of wisdom for each of them to discover.

What was her message for Nina?

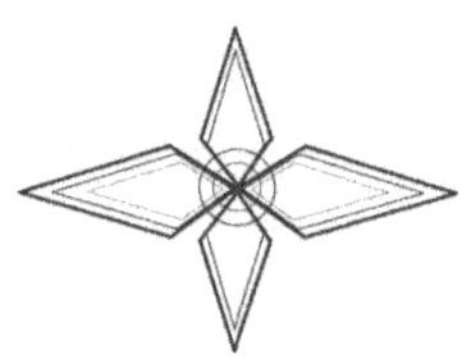

THIRTEEN

Before they made their way out to the pink grass field, Grandma Ova checked on Zeycott's leg and gave them a thumbs-up.

"I don't need the cane." Zeycott gave it back to Grandma Ova.

Nina piped up. "Are you sure that's a good idea?"

"I can walk fine without the cane. I just had it with me to ease your mind."

"What if you limp?"

Zeycott placed a hand on either side of her shoulders. "Then I'll lean on you for help."

She rolled her eyes. That would have been fine, except that she was half his size.

Grandma Ova took the cane and put it in the closet. "He'll be fine without the cane, Nina."

She turned to Zeycott. "Let me know as soon as something hurts, okay?"

"I will. You took Grandma Ova's words over mine."

"It's because you're a male. You think you're invincible

when you're not." Nina caught sight of Grandma's gaze and winked. Nina patted the pocket on her shirt that concealed a device she had borrowed from Grandma Ova.

"Who said that?" Zeycott scrunched his face.

"Just basic knowledge of the male species, no matter what galaxy they're from. C'mon, let's get going before it gets too late."

They strode out of the house and headed toward the pink grass. She watched Zeycott walk on the dirt trail and when he didn't show any discomfort, she relaxed.

"Your recovery is faster than that of a healing paper cut. Seriously." She stopped in her steps and faced him. "Yesterday, I saw your leg . . . bent in the most awkward position."

"You mean deformed."

She huffed out a sigh. "I didn't want to use that word. It has a bad connotation. I'll never forget that image and how it made me feel."

He tipped up her chin. "I know how it made you feel. When the Ulkrins attacked you, I felt the same way. I was terrified."

"In less than a day, your bones have fused together with new bone growth. You're walking like nothing happened." She glanced down at his knee. "It's incredible. I can only imagine how this kind of cutting-edge medicine would benefit humans on Earth. It could save so many lives."

"It could," he said. "If there were a million Ninas around."

"What do you mean?"

"There's only one of you, and you're mine." He bent down to kiss her lightly on the lips. "Don't forget, *you* are the reason I'm standing here. You said it yourself. Your energy sparked the healing in my bones. It literally sparked." He laughed. "I felt the electricity running through me each time it happened. It's crazy and thrilling. Every time I'm near you, I die a little, but you're worth every spark of pain."

"I don't want to hear the word 'die' associated with you, okay? You're *not* dying."

"Even if I was, you're worth it."

She rose to her toes and kissed him on the cheek. "When does the spark happen? Is it random?"

"It's when I want you."

"Oh." A simple word that pulsed with anticipation and wonder. That meant he'd wanted her all those times she thought he'd loathed her.

They both left it at that as they continued down a pebble path illuminated with small glowing flowers. That path opened to a magnificent field of tall pink grass with a lovely swarm of blue fireflies. A gentle breeze brushed by, sending the grass swaying. The tips of the grass glittered like an ocean of stars.

Nina reached for a blade of grass, bent it over, and ran a finger down its surface. The softness surprised her. She released it, and it sprung back. Her mind eased, and her muscles relaxed as she inhaled and exhaled the grass's sweet fragrance. She hadn't been this calm in a long time.

"I can't believe how healing it is just to walk through pink grass." She fell in step with Zeycott. "How are you feeling? Is the fresh air helping you at all?"

The corners of his eyes crinkled, and she could see the reflection of the glittering grass in them. "I'm feeling wonderful. I'm not saying that just to make you feel better. It's the truth. Taking a stroll with you tonight escalated my healing even more." He grabbed her hand. "Let's go find a spot to sit and stargaze. I've always wanted to do this with you."

Zeycott led the way to a sloped hill that overlooked an enormous field of grass that went on and on. The glow made it appear like a sea of pink stars were at her feet. She sensed all distractions shedding from her body as though the blades of grass scraped off the nasty crust that had clung to her today.

They found a spot with glowing flowers by a hillside and sat down, the pink grass becoming their backdrop and the starry sky their ceiling. She could fall asleep to this beautiful view.

"Let me check your knee one more time." Nina dug into her pocket and pulled out a portable x-ray scanner she had borrowed from Grandma Ova. It was made from metal and crystal that transferred the information to her smart ring.

Curiosity had her wanting to learn about Zeycott's bone development. How were his bones growing back so quickly? What did they look like when they sparked inside his body? Were the bones blue everywhere, or did it affect certain areas? The whole concept intrigued her.

She waved the portable x-ray scanner in front of him. "Is it okay for me to examine your bones?"

Zeycott shot her an amused look. "*He's* always looking for an examination." He gestured to his friend, an obvious bulge making his presence known through the loose clothing from Grandma Ova.

Heat blossomed on her cheeks. She didn't even know why she blushed so easily around him. All he had to do was look at her and her body responded.

Though she would love to take advantage of the romantic

ambience and continue their yoga sex session, she wanted him to heal, to rest.

"That 'bone' is a different study for another time." She laid a hand on his chest. "It fascinates me how my energy inspired your body to heal. It matters to me how I affect you."

Zeycott stretched out his legs and leaned back with his hands, taking on a relaxed position. "Examine away. After you satisfy your curiosity, I want to know when you first saw my mist."

Nina pulled up a screen on the x-ray scanner. She held the device about five inches from his body, starting from the top of his head, and scanned downward. She took her time around his shoulders, chest, and arms. The bones were all blue. She paused at the injured area, allowing the scanner to take in more details. When she passed his tented arousal, it twitched, and he sucked in a breath. Ignoring him, she moved the scanner down his thighs, calves, and to his feet. She turned off the x-ray device and expanded her virtual screen to review the close-ups.

She gasped when she saw the bones around his shoulders and chest. "Oh my God." She gaped at him. "How is this possible? How are there images on your bones? Who put them there? What are they?"

Nina had never seen images etched on the bones of a living body. The intricate designs on Zeycott's bones were mostly on his shoulders and arms. The art had a silver glitter, which became more pronounced due to the blue contrast of his bones.

She stared in awe at the images and words that made her think of emojis from her mobile phone on Earth. She made out his name neatly hidden inside an abstract design.

"They're tattoos I put on myself a while ago."

Tattoos? Nina's eyes widened. "You have machines that could ink your bones?"

The technology on this planet never flabbergasted her.

"There are various kinds of tattoos you can get," he said. "I created the device to ink on bones because there were none available when I wanted to do it. I sold the technology to a company to reproduce it for the public. It's a specialized technique and a very expensive machine. Those who want to ink themselves usually want their art to be seen, not hidden in their bones."

Nina ran a hand down his shoulder. "Does it hurt?"

"Emotional pain hurts more than physical pain, so sending a laser beam into my bones was tolerable. Plus, there are numbing agents I take before the procedure to help ease the discomfort."

What kind of emotional pain had he endured? She moved her hand over to his heart. "Who hurt you?"

He covered her hand with his. "Remember when you asked me about the scars on my shoulders and chest?"

She nodded, and he took off his shirt, revealing the tattoos she had admired. Her fingers traced the scars hidden by the art. She didn't know why, but she pressed her lips to them, wanting to erase the agony that had caused them.

He hitched a breath. "Nina."

"I don't want you hurting anymore," she said.

"No one has cared for me like this."

"That's because you've been waiting for me."

They had been waiting for each other.

A sudden look of regret passed his contemplative face. "There was a chemical explosion during one of my rescue missions. I got injured trying to save a family." He swallowed. "They didn't make it. The chemical melted my skin. I got the tattoos to cover up the deformity. Every time I see the scars, it reminds me of how I failed."

Nina twisted her lips, unsure how to soothe him. "I'm sorry to hear that. You did your best. Sometimes, life doesn't happen the way you want it to. But don't forget that you *didn't* fail at saving me and my sisters." She traced the scars with her fingers. "I don't think this is a deformity. You've turned sorrow into art on your body. When I look at it, I see beauty. But now that I know its story, it gives the tattoos more depth and meaning."

His lips tilted. "Thank you. I knew there was a reason I was attracted to you. You make me feel valuable."

"The feeling is mutual."

In the soft light from the glowing grass and flowers, his tattoos fluctuated. Nina blinked, believing her eyes were playing tricks on her. Intrigued, she shifted her position, sitting upright and running her fingers along the abstract designs again. As she did so, the ink moved, transforming the artwork into words from the universal language. *Love, peace, and forgiveness.* The words flowed over his skin.

She couldn't take her eyes away from the mutable art. "Do all tattoos in Saedo move like this? I didn't see them move on you before. Why is it moving now?"

"The ink responds to emotions. Sometimes they move, sometimes they don't. You have a knack for making my body react like no one else."

"It's because we're made for each other." She poked at him playfully.

"We have all kinds of high-tech ink that can do various

things. But this ink was from the Saedo cedrus tree in combination with motion properties. When you're ready for your tattoo, I can use this type of ink if you'd like."

Nina hadn't even thought about what she'd want, but the idea of having moving art on her body intrigued her. "That would be cool. What about the ink on your bones? What inspired you to do that?"

Zeycott lifted a shoulder. "When you die, your flesh decomposes, but your bones will remain. I guess I just wanted to share my 'story' with the soil and the land when I'm gone."

"That sounds really sad . . . and really beautiful." Her heart ached for him.

His message was profound. He wanted his life to mean something. This disease had given him a different perspective on life, and in doing so, he had revealed another layer of himself to her.

She wished she had met him sooner, so he wasn't so lonely. He had probably lived with fear and hopelessness for so long, wondering when the disease would take his last breath. She wanted to wipe that darkness from him. She wanted to give him all the joy and love he deserved.

With that kind of dark cloud hovering over him, how did he maintain a relationship? It must have been difficult.

"Have you dated a lot?"

Zeycott sat forward. "Not seriously. We'd always go into the relationship knowing that it was just sex. I made the rules clear from the beginning."

"Oh." She nibbled on the inside of her mouth, thinking. "But you didn't set out any rules with me."

"You're not like everyone else. You're my catalyst. You

broke every rule I ever had." He wrapped an arm around her. "I couldn't stop myself from wanting you. I didn't know why then, but I know now. I can't imagine not being with you."

But I could die, and I don't want to hurt you. She heard the words he didn't say.

As she stared at the virtual screen showing the tattoos on his bones, tears welled in her eyes. But she pushed them down, not wanting him to think she pitied him.

She wanted to give him hope. "Like you said, I'm the catalyst, and that means I'm going to *cure* you."

She'd find a way. She refused to believe the Universe would be this mean to her. Why would it gift her this marvelous star-being if it was just going to take him away from her?

No, she did not believe that.

Nina returned her attention to the x-ray scans and skipped to the video of his injured knee. She zoomed in for more details. She had never been one of those people who enjoyed looking at things under the microscope. Science was science. She didn't need to know the details of how things functioned, but being on a new planet had changed her.

Being in love had *transformed* her. Love. Her heart thundered from the admission. She took a moment to let the profound truth settle in. It dropped like a pebble and descended slowly into the well of her soul. The remarkable effect rippled throughout her body, stimulating each bodily system, and making her extremely aware of her senses. Even her heartbeat echoed in her ears like a sacred song.

Once it settled, fear squirmed in her. She had more to lose now. Zeycott was too important to her. She didn't want to think about the inevitable, so she shoved the thought away.

Right now, she was enjoying an evening with her lover, a green star-being who literally sparked for her. Nothing else mattered but this magical moment.

"What does it feel like when your bone sparks?" she asked. "Can you sense your bones behaving differently now that they're blue?"

"Like an electrical shock that emanates to every other bone in my body, sort of like a shockwave. As for the color, I haven't noticed anything abnormal. I've been too focused on the spark and you."

A quiet snap occurred, and she glanced over at his chest. "Was that a spark?"

He nodded, rubbing his sternum.

"That's incredible. I didn't know it made an actual sound." She looked at him, and his sage-colored eyes darkened. "Are you feeling okay?"

"I'm used to it now. You can hear it when the surroundings are quiet. Tell me when you first saw my mist."

"At the marketplace gallery. I didn't know it was yours. The mist kept showing up after that day."

"That makes sense now. I helped set up the fossil display for the gallery. The bones of the Saedo cat have remnants of mine."

Life was full of little surprises that somehow connected to each other. She thought back on those times when she noticed Zeycott with gorgeous star-beings and wondered if he ever saw her.

"I didn't think you noticed me. Beautiful females always surrounded you."

"Oh, I saw you, Nina." He skimmed his fingers down her spine and heat pooled at her core. "I also noticed that the other soldiers saw you. I told them to leave you alone because you prefer females."

"What?!" She shoved at him. "You did not! I mean, there's nothing wrong with that if it were true. What's wrong with you?"

"*You.*" He laughed. "I did what I had to do to keep them away from you. I know it was selfish of me, but that was my instinctive reaction."

"I can't believe you." She narrowed her eyes into slits. "I'm going to start a rumor that you prefer men now . . . no, you prefer horrific creatures with pink fur and sparkly tails that speak with an annoying voice."

With a smile, he shrugged. "Okay. Fair enough. I don't care what anyone thinks. I only care what you think of me." His fingers continued skating down her back and settled above her waistband. "What do you think of me?"

Desire slicked between her legs. *Be good. Behave,* she scolded her body. She should enjoy a simple night stargazing with him and nothing more.

"I think you're the most incredible man I've ever met. Green is my favorite color now, especially this shade on you." She patted his cheek. "I also love the variations of sage in your eyes."

"Keep going." Zeycott nipped at her earlobe. "Do you want me?"

"No . . ."

He should rest, but her body yearned for his addictive mouth as he nibbled down to her neck. She turned, giving him full access.

"Don't lie to me, Nina. Do you want me?" The rumble of his voice against her skin made her tingle.

When his hand lowered and claimed a buttock, she blurted out, "Yes. I want you."

Traitor. She needed to have a serious talk with her body another time. Right now, all she could do was let the overwhelming passion roll through her.

"I want you too." He growled, shifting his body so he could cradle her. Muscular arms wrapped around her, making her feel warm and safe.

As much as she wanted him right now, she needed him to recover more. She searched for coherent words within her discombobulated brain. "I know what you want. I want it too. But not tonight, handsome. I want you to heal, *need* you to be well." She kissed his cheek and pointed to the night sky. "I've never spent the night outside stargazing. Want to? The fragrant grass would be good for both of us."

His expression softened. "Okay."

She snuggled into the crook of his chest. His warmth blanketed her, and his musky scent made her feel at home.

The crickets sang a soothing song. The breeze sent a sweet aroma to her nose, and his body embraced her as she drifted off into a trance-inducing state. "I can't keep my eyes open."

"Sleep." He brushed strands of curly hair away from her face.

Somewhere in her dream, she heard him say, "I love you."

FOURTEEN

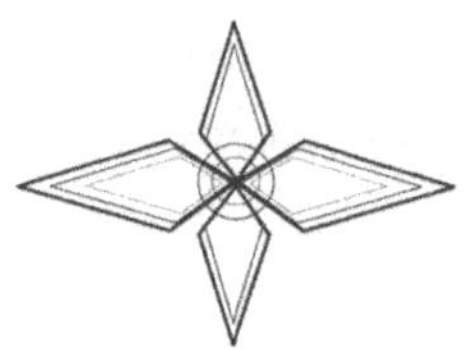

Nina woke to voices. She opened her eyes, and the ocean of stars glittered in the dark sky. The midnight blue that draped above her had a pink tint, signifying that dawn would arrive soon. She checked her smart ring. The time showed three in the morning. The pink grass glowed around her like a night lantern that offered her just enough illumination.

Beside her, Zeycott's legs tangled with hers. Her body ached a little from the hard surface of the ground, but it was worth it. She'd never slept outside like this. Perhaps they could bring sleeping bags or even set up a tent for next time.

Voices echoed again, reminding her why she had woken up. She gently removed Zeycott's leg from crushing hers. She blinked the sleep from her eyes and glanced around, but didn't see anyone.

She yawned, stretched out her arms, and rose from the ground. Voices boomed again, this time louder. Her body shivered from a chill that didn't come from the morning air. She didn't know how she knew that.

Her heart dropped when a translucent image fluctuated about twenty feet from her. Waves of energy flashed and dimmed, making the image appear like it was behind a fuzzy lens. Could it be Zeycott's mom trying to connect to her again? Nina kept her eyes on the augmenting energy, but no ancestors appeared.

A sliver of orange mist flowed across Nina, circulating the image as though it wanted her to focus on it. She waited for Surell to appear, but no one surfaced. What were the ancestors trying to tell her?

When the mist disappeared, a blue firefly flew past her and into the wave of energy that expanded from the ground to the pink grass. A hiss rang out, and the bug flashed like something had zapped it. She could still see the bug flying around, but its image blurred like it was behind an energy curtain. Was she looking at a portal?

Gravelly voices boomed, and the image shifted like the frequency of the voices penetrating a veil. The eerie sounds intruded the peaceful environment, and the luminosity of the pink grass dimmed, and blades stopped swaying as though it sensed foreign energy. What was she looking at? Nina moved closer for a better view, but stayed in the shadows by the rocks.

Nina crouched as she tried to see something from the blurry image. It was hard to tell when the image kept moving back and forth like fabric in the wind. More growls erupted from the image and boomed right into her ear.

The blue firefly flew around the image and out back toward her. Energy snapped, and the fuzziness cleared as though someone adjusted the focus on a camera lens, revealing a clear image of a tunnel. Not only that but she could also see trees, rocks, the dawn peeking through the horizon as though someone was showing her a movie, panning from one angle to another. Maybe the firefly shifted something.

This is a portal. Something warm brushed her hand. She glanced down to see a small sliver of orange mist with sparkles around her wrist, a confirmation of what she was looking at.

She stared at the image as it showed her a wooded area. When two Ulkrins and their beasts wandered into view, terror spiked in her. She clasped a hand over her mouth to prevent the loud shriek that wanted to come.

She was about to whirl around to wake up Zeycott when an Ulkrin wearing a dark metallic armor with blades along his sleeves appeared. She watched him like a movie on a screen. Something about him froze her in place. He had chin-length dark hair that covered part of his face, and he was larger than the other Ulkrins. He spoke to the Ulkrin soldiers that were decked in gray and brown uniforms. They reminded her of the heinous aliens who had abducted her.

"I have the Silver Text. It was hidden inside the tattoo place. Find the other one."

No, no no! She needed that tablet!

Fear squirmed in Nina's stomach, and she turned back in Zeycott's direction. Her foot stepped on a dry blade of grass. It crunched beneath her shoes. *Shit.* The sound echoed, making its presence known in the otherwise silent field. Nina crouched lower, uncertain if they could see her.

"Did you hear that?" one of the Ulkrins asked.

"Probably a spider or some rodent. I just killed a rat earlier," someone replied.

She peered over the rock and saw the Ulkrins glancing around, but not in her direction. They could hear her, but could they see her?

Nina moved closer, but stayed in the shadows as best she could. A foot away from the portal, she could see the difference in energies. A glittery curtain lay over the portal. She extended her hand in front of it and waved. No comment from the Ulkrins. So they couldn't see her, but they could hear her.

Someone with heavy feet approached. "Commander Kruegen, another female has died. We're tossing her into the burner." The snarling voice appeared so close.

She wanted to scream for Zeycott, but feared the Ulkrins would hear her.

"Head back to the control center now. I need to dissect this tablet." Commander Kruegen flipped over the rectangular brown tablet and studied it. "Continue with the experiments while I extract the data. Saedo will die for stealing our humans."

Was he referring to her and her sisters, or other humans?

The portal zoomed in for her. "Yes, Commander Kruegen." The Ulkrin soldier smiled, revealing fangs caked with grime. "We'll seek retribution for the murder of Commander Ooza."

Commander Kruegen growled and clenched his fist. "He died for the Ulkrin Mission. He won't be forgotten."

"I'll rip them apart and feed them to my offspring." A mother Ulkrin beast snarled and curled her tail around Commander Kruegen.

Commander Kruegen nodded and started down a tunnel. Nina's heart raced when she recognized the rocky walls. She'd seen them when Zeycott and his brothers had discussed an Ulkrin portal being left open.

Zeycott mentioned his brothers had installed hidden devices in and around the tunnel to monitor them. Was anyone watching this at the control center?

She couldn't let the Ulkrin leave with the Silver Text tablet. That was Zeycott's only chance of survival! She whirled and whispered his name, "Zeycott."

She tried her best to keep her voice down. He didn't move, and she sent him a message to his wristband.

Going after Ulkrin. Following tunnel. They have Silver Text. Can't let them take it. Must save you.

She swallowed her dry throat and stepped closer to the translucent image that had expanded before her. She reached out a hand, touched the image, and penetrated the cool surface. When her fingers went through, electricity hissed and flashed. The portal faded, and she couldn't hear the Ulkrins anymore.

She retracted her hand, glancing back at Zeycott once more. He was still sound asleep. A nearby pebble caught her eye. She picked it up and pitched it at him, aiming for his back, but it landed on his butt.

He shifted.

"Zeycott! Wake up!" she whispered.

She couldn't let the Ulkrins get away with the Silver Text. She had to go *now*. She stepped through the portal, and a powerful force sucked her in.

"Nina!"

She looked over her shoulder as Zeycott rushed forward, reaching for her. She extended her hand to him, but the portal faded, shrank, and cut him off from view.

"No!" Zeycott's voice echoed as Nina stood alone in the dark tunnel, lit with haphazard lights attached to the ceiling.

FIFTEEN

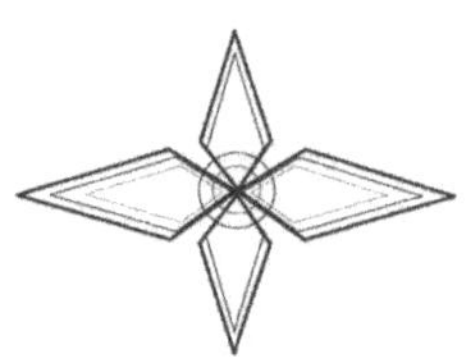

The reality of what had just happened settled in for Nina. She inhaled a deep breath to ground herself, grasping for courage.

Be brave, Nina. You're doing this for Zeycott. He needs you. You need him.

She took in a few more breaths, exhaled, and pushed terror aside. *Go away.*

She had to retrieve the Silver Text for the star-being who had rescued her and her heart. She could do this for him. The idea that she could fail and die flashed in her mind, but she didn't entertain it.

Nina checked her smart ring, but she couldn't seem to get any reception. Regardless, she took images of her surroundings and sent them to Zeycott for reference. Was this the same tunnel she had seen from the map Zeycott had discussed with his brothers? Or was this tunnel one of many accessible from the Ulkrin portal? It didn't matter; the images would help him locate her.

Nina moved along the side of the tunnel, keeping her eyes and ears open. Where did Commander Kruegen go?

She came to a fork. Each path looked the same. "Ugh, shit. Which way?"

She braced a hand on the wall, looking down at the dirt for footprints. The skin on her hand tickled, and she glanced over.

"Ah!" She clamped a hand over her mouth as soon as her cry eked out.

A large fuzzy white spider with over eight eyes skittered onto her hand, lingering. It had ten legs and a body the size of her fist. She froze and let it move across her hand onto the wall and down to the ground. Fear skated down her body as the spider scurried this way and that way, looking deadly. Was it poisonous?

She had an aversion to spiders, not an outright phobia, but close enough. They didn't elicit a panic attack in her; she just thought they were nasty. Her skin crawled whenever she saw one.

The white spider sniffed or made a sound similar to it as it crawled toward the path on the right. Then it stopped. A brown spider with dark spots crawled out from a hole in the ground. It was twice the size of the white one. A hissing war erupted between the two spiders.

Nina didn't need this right now. She had to go find the Ulkrins, but these horrendous spiders were having some kind of spider war.

The brown spider shot out some tar-like thing from its giant glinting fangs. The tar moved on the ground, forming little pools of blackness that shifted into various shapes. The white spider dodged the moveable tar and released a silver liquid that wrapped around the sticky blackness. Flashes burst, and the tar disintegrated into vapor that disappeared into the air. The brown spider hissed and crawled back into its hole.

As if nothing had happened, the white spider continued its way down the path. Something told Nina she should follow it. This creature seemed to know the "safe" path. Animals and bugs had instincts that humans didn't. She prayed she chose the right decision to trust this spider—an arachnid that gave her the heebie-jeebies. If she had more time to spare, that logic to trust something that terrified her made little sense.

As she made her way further down the path, voices began to echo in the corridor. They were cries for help, coming from a room with a metal door, which the white spider crawled under.

Nina heard footsteps approach. She yanked on the brass doorknob, held her breath, and turned. When the door opened, she blew out a sigh of relief, entered, and closed the door gently. A metallic smell hit her nose, and she glanced around the room lit by a small light on the opposite wall. Two beds lined a wall with immobile bodies under blankets. Something told her they were dead. A third bed was in the dark corner, but some large machine blocked it from view.

Ulkrin soldiers strode by outside of the room, and Nina remained against the wall beside a window with curtains that gave her a peek of the beasts. As they passed, the Ulkrins spoke about human captives. Had they captured more humans?

A sick feeling settled into the pit of her stomach. She remembered the terror that had frightened her and her sisters. They were fortunate to have had the soldiers of Saedo rescue them. Where were these captives? Was anyone helping them?

"Please help me," said a small voice in the room.

Nina made her way to the corner and around the beeping machine. A dark-haired woman pushed herself up to sit on the edge of the bed and flicked on the light beside her bed. With enough lighting, Nina could see everything in the room, especially the blood on the other two beds. This human woman wore a roomy white gown that revealed her sharp collar bones. Bruises covered her pale boney arms and neck. She had hollow cheeks, dark circles under her eyes, and dry, cracked lips. Spots of dried blood clung to her ankles and feet. She was breastfeeding a gray-skinned baby with a dark patch of hair.

Oh, no. One look at the baby told her it was a human-alien hybrid.

The woman shifted, winced, and a pillow fell. She tried to reach for it with a trembling hand, but winced in pain.

"Let me get that for you." Nina picked up the pillow and placed it back against the wall.

"Thank you," the fragile woman replied and touched Nina's face gently. "Are you a new captive?"

"No, I'm not."

"Oh." Hope glimmered in her eyes, even though she looked pale as a ghost. Her baby squirmed and cried, and she soothed it with a slight bounce of her arm. With each bounce, she winced.

"Are you all right?" Nina asked.

"No, I'm not." She gestured to the other two beds. She couldn't see the bodies clearly as the lights around their beds were off. "They died during birth. Their babies died too."

Nina cursed out loud. What the hell was this place?

"I'm Nina. What's your name?"

"Amelia." She reached for a glass of water by the bedside, but her hand trembled too much. "Can you help me? I might drop it."

"Of course." Nina grabbed the glass and helped her take a few gulps.

"Thank you. I need fluids to help feed him." She smiled at her baby, who gurgled happily. His eyes opened and glanced around.

"How many of you were abducted?"

"I'm not sure," Amelia said. "There were others here before me. These aliens are experimenting on us. They're impregnating us with some kind of device. This is my baby boy." Her face softened with love. "They call him UB20, Ulkrin Baby 20." Tears welled in her eyes. "But he's Benjamin to me."

"Benjamin is adorable. Look at his smile," Nina said as the baby yawned and settled into a sweet smile, his eyes closing again.

Amelia licked her dry lips. "I know you don't know me, and we've just met, but I need a favor from you."

Nina placed a gentle hand on Amelia's arm. "I'll try my best to get you out of here."

Amelia shook her head. "No, I won't make it. I don't have energy to move. Whatever energy I have left is saved to feed Benjamin. I'm still bleeding on and off since giving birth. My body won't make it. I'll just be extra weight dragging you down." She looked at Nina with pleading eyes. "Can you please save him? He's innocent and full of life. My beautiful boy." She brushed her finger across a small stain on his forehead. "He even has this cute little birthmark. I've always wanted a baby, and he's my miracle. He doesn't look evil to me."

No, the baby wasn't evil. He looked precious with his chubby cheeks and brown eyes that looked so much like his mom's. Nina could take Benjamin with her, but she didn't know her way out. The portal had closed, and she couldn't go back to it if she wanted to. She didn't want to make a promise she couldn't keep, so she delivered the truth.

"I want Benjamin safe, and I want to help you, but I'm not sure how to get out of here. Or if I'll make it out alive. I came here through a portal, and I don't know if there's another way to escape. I'm looking for Commander Kruegen. He stole something from my friends, and I need it back."

"I know the way out. I can show you. I've been in here for five months. Benjamin will die in their hands. Who knows what other experiments they'll do on him? I'd rather take my chances with you. Please."

Nina nodded. "Okay." She would do her best to get Benjamin to safety. "Where is this place?"

Amelia shrugged. "I don't know. I just know it's underground. There are many tunnels, and they all look similar. There are Ulkrin soldiers and beasts everywhere. But right now, they're in a meeting, which is why it's quiet. But once it's over, they'll be back in here. You need to leave soon. Commander Kruegen is ruthless—well, they all are—but he's smarter, which makes him more dangerous. I've witnessed his interaction with other Ulkrins when they first brought me here with the other girls. He doesn't visit in these rooms. Only the soldiers and nurses come and go in here."

"Does he have an office? I need to track him down."

Nina didn't know if he would have the tablet with him or placed it somewhere safe. She prayed he left it somewhere to attend the meeting. She had little time if the Ulkrin meeting would end soon. Her escape window narrowed. She glanced at her smart ring, and a message from Zeycott splashed on the screen.

We're on our way. Stay hidden if you can.

Nina looked up at Amelia. "Is it okay if I snap a picture of Benjamin? My friends are coming. I want them to make Benjamin's safety a priority."

Hope gleamed in Amelia's eyes. "Yes, of course."

After Nina took the image, she sent Zeycott a message. *This baby needs protection. Please keep him safe too. There are human captives here.*

"Commander Kruegen's office is in the corner, past the nursery. They have a nurse who comes in to check on me and Benjamin every few hours. She wears a hooded cloak like that over there. You can wear it." Amelia jerked her chin to the brown thing hanging over a chair by one of the deceased bodies.

"Are they going to remove these bodies?" Nina asked, wondering how long they had been dead. A decomposed body would threaten the health of both Amelia and the baby.

"Silvia and Brenda just passed yesterday. The Ulkrins took their babies away. I'm not sure when they're coming back for them. I didn't know them until I came to this room."

Nina could only imagine Amelia's terror. She desperately

wanted to help her and her little boy escape. "I'll be back for you."

Just as Nina prepared to leave, the white spider crawled up her leg. "Oh, shit." Her heart hammered in her chest. *Not right now.*

"I've seen that spider before. I don't think it's vicious," Amelia said. "I overheard the Ulkrin soldiers call it White Mutaat. It's rare, or something like that. I forgot what they said."

Nina cringed. "You didn't see how it killed the brown spider."

"Oh, that one's venomous." Amelia didn't even flinch when the white spider scurried over to her arm, close to the baby. *Too close to the baby.* "There are a lot of spiders and other bugs in this place."

The White Mutaat spider crawled back to Nina's body, clinging to the hem of her shirt before scurrying into the baggy pocket. "Eww." Goosebumps bloomed on her skin. She didn't want to touch the spider, but she also didn't want it in her pocket. "You sure it's not poisonous?"

"I don't know, but these aliens let it wander around. They killed one of those brown ones the other day, so if this white spider is poisonous, they would have killed it too." Amelia peeked into Nina's shirt pocket. "I think it likes you."

Nina would be more relieved if it left her alone. She peered inside her pocket and several eyes stared back at her. Time wasn't on her side, so she shoved the heebie-jeebies aside.

She went over to the chair, grabbed the brown cloak, and put it on. The wide hood covered her face well.

Amelia pointed to a side door. "Go through there, then

take a right and another right. His office has weapons attached to his door. Be careful—there are cameras on the ceiling. There's a tunnel beyond his office that leads to the outside. They took me and the girls out once for fresh air after implanting us."

She and her sisters could have been here . . . She shivered and forced herself not to think about it. She needed courage right now, not fear.

Nina ran a gentle hand over Benjamin's face and met Amelia's eyes. "I'll be back for both of you. I have to retrieve something first."

The idea that Nina could fail weighed heavily on her mind, but she didn't want to give Amelia more anxiety.

Though Amelia looked pale and fragile, she smiled. Nina meant what she said. She wouldn't abandon Amelia and her baby here.

With a thumping heart, Nina inhaled a deep breath. *You can do this. You can do this.*

Zeycott's face splashed in her vision. He had looked frightened when he had reached for her but couldn't get through. Knowing that he was on his way gave her the strength to hurry.

Nina pulled the cloak over her head and exited through the side door. The hallway was brighter than the tunnel. She walked slowly on the stone pathway, keeping her face to the ground, avoiding the cameras above.

She strode by the nursery and peeked through the window. From a cursory glance, she didn't see any babies. She spotted a black door with a wreath of knives attached to the front.

Nerves twisted in her stomach. She closed her eyes for a

second and imagined Zeycott's embrace. He had given her what she'd lacked. He made her feel worthy, loved. She wanted the same for him. She had to retrieve the Silver Text for him, had to cure him. He deserved a healthy and happy life.

Seeing Zeycott's face settled her nerves. Nina waited a beat, listened, and when she didn't hear anyone from the inside, she grabbed the metal doorknob and entered. It surprised her that the door wasn't locked. The Ulkrins probably didn't think any intruders would dare wander their halls.

Two virtual monitors splashed above a black desk when it sensed her presence. Her heart leaped when she spotted the brown tablet she had seen Commander Kruegen examine through the portal. Up close, the Silver Text had a glassy effect on the surface. It looked like a flat gemstone. It sat on the desk, hooked up to some cord that was attached to another machine.

He was probably trying to extract data from it. Nina glanced at the screen and saw a series of codes running up and down. She didn't contemplate further. She yanked the cord out and clasped the Silver Text. Heat bloomed upon contact. Or was that just the heat of adrenaline and fear jumbled together in her body?

Orange mist with silver sparks appeared and flowed around her. Was that a sign that Zeycott was nearby? She tucked the Silver Text into her other baggy pocket. She'd almost forgotten about the White Mutaat. It peeked out from the pocket, hissed, and returned inside.

Nina rushed back to Amelia. "I got it. We should all go now."

Amelia tried to get up, winced, and wobbled. "I'm too

weak. Please, just take Benjamin. I'd be forever grateful." She handed the baby over to Nina.

Angry noises echoed through the halls.

"Go now. They're back." Amelia nudged Nina toward the side door. "Go! I won't make it. They've done horrible things to my body. It's only a matter of time before I succumb to those injuries. Please keep Benjamin safe for me. Let him know that I love him."

Nina's heart broke for her, and tears spilled over. She nodded and left the room.

"We have an intruder. Find her!" an Ulkrin snarled.

Feet stomped and angry shouts erupted. She ran past Commander Kruegen's office. There was a corridor to her left and right. The orange mist flowed down the corridor to the right and rounded a corner. Nina followed, arrived at a door, and pushed it.

It didn't open.

Shit, shit, shit! Fear tumbled inside her as she whipped around, searching for another way to escape. She held the baby tighter.

Growls and footsteps approached closer. She pushed and kicked at the door, but it wouldn't budge. The White Mutaat hopped out of her pocket and wrapped its legs around the doorknob. Silver liquid excreted from its fangs and enveloped the doorknob. The doorknob disintegrated, and the spider hissed and jumped back into her pocket.

"Get her!" Commander Kruegen shouted at his army of Ulkrin soldiers.

SIXTEEN

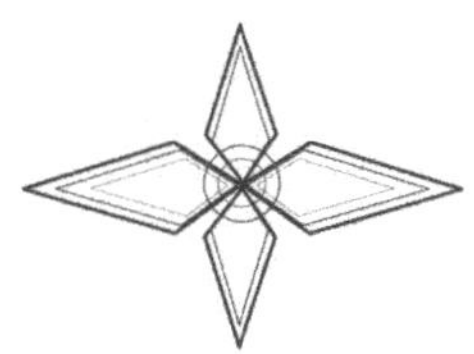

Nina kicked the door again, and it flew open. She ran out to a wooded area. Sunlight streamed down from above, mimicking sharp blades cutting into the dark.

Blasts boomed, and she jumped, embracing baby Benjamin closer. She glanced over her shoulder, and Ulkrin soldiers and beasts poured out, chasing after her.

"Nina! Over here!"

She whirled toward Zeycott's voice. Dressed in black armor, he fired at the Ulkrins with a massive blaster. Bodies fell, giving Nina some relief from the enemies. In the distance, three longships, several autobuses, and other emergency vehicles flashed.

Soldiers poured out of a dark longship made from reflective glass. She recognized Raeko, Maeson, Osayik, Arkon, and Jarzell. More soldiers emerged, but she didn't know them.

"Take her to safety." Raeko nodded to Zeycott. "We've got this."

Raeko signaled to his brothers. They separated into three groups and surrounded the cave she exited from.

"You hurt?" Zeycott surveyed her.

"No. How are you feeling?" Nina scanned his face and didn't see any signs of discomfort. She was ecstatic to see him, but feared the combat could injure him. The disease was still active inside him. He hadn't been cured yet, which meant his condition was unpredictable.

He let out a short laugh. "You're worried about me? I'm better now that I know you're okay. Let's get you out of here." He led her back to the emergency crew beside the autobuses, which were like longer, more spacious ambulances. They came equipped with state-of-the-art technology that could serve as emergency rooms on the move.

Zeycott gawked at the baby, who opened his eyes and burped. "Is that an Ulkrin baby?"

"Mixed race. He's human and Ulkrin." Nina clasped his arm. "Benjamin's mom is still in there. Her name is Amelia. Can you please ask your brothers to rescue her too? She could've been me and my sisters."

He nodded, pulled up a screen from his wristband, and delivered the message.

"I can take the baby and make sure he's okay. My name is Bekka." A purple-haired female medic dressed in white held out her arms to Nina.

Nina transferred Benjamin over and watched as Bekka placed him on a small table where four padded walls came up, creating a protective border around the baby.

Zeycott pulled Nina in for a tight embrace. "We'll talk when I get back. I need to go help my brothers. Bekka will take you back to the Village Center first. I want you safe." He kissed her forehead.

"Be careful." Nina linked her fingers with his. "You shouldn't even be here fighting. Your knee, your leg, your bones—"

"You think I can stay back while *you*—a yoga instructor who's not used to combat—try to save *me*?" The space between his eyebrows creased. "You almost gave me a corra attack. Don't do that again. I'll die from worrying about you before the disease ever gets to me. We'll talk about your lack of judgment when this is over." He sighed and lifted her hand to his lips. "Stay here and *don't* go anywhere. Promise?"

Lack of judgment? She didn't like his words. His condescending tone pierced her heart. Why would he say something like that? She did what she *thought* was best. She went after Ulkrins for *him*! Maybe she should *reevaluate* her judgment in men. She fumed, but was too tired to entertain the anger. She didn't have the energy for it.

Nina watched as Zeycott joined his brothers in battle. Blasts boomed, and her stomach lurched, fearing for their safety. These star-beings were her family. They had rescued her—*twice*.

Despite Zeycott's inconsiderate words, she was grateful he'd arrived at a critical moment. Nina dropped down next to baby Benjamin and considered the complexity and beauty of what this infant symbolized for the future. He was half-human and half-alien—the malicious kind. But this cute and innocent face didn't depict an ounce of darkness. Children were all born innocent, no matter where they came from. No matter if they were humans, aliens, or animals.

Benjamin cooed when Bekka changed his diaper, dressed

him in a new onesie, and covered his head with a cheerful green hat. The little birthmark on his forehead was more visible now that he'd been cleaned. Bekka swaddled him in a soft blanket that made him look like a colorful burrito.

Something moved in her pocket, and then she remembered. Goosebumps formed on her skin. The White Mutaat snuck out of from her pocket and peered at her.

You can go now, she told it telepathically.

It ducked back into her pocket. If Nina weren't so fatigued, she'd find tongs or something to take it elsewhere.

Her hand gripped the tablet from inside the other pocket. The Silver Text was now in her hands, and that meant she could save Zeycott.

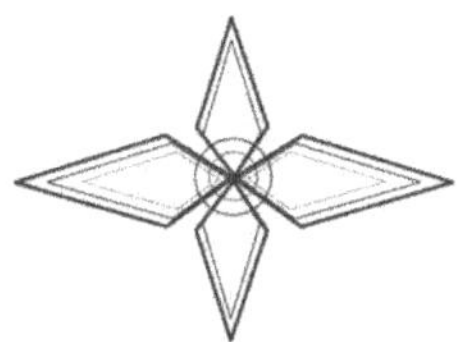

SEVENTEEN

A few hours later, the pediatric care team at the Village Center Hospital examined baby Benjamin. Her sister Isabella had worked as a pediatric nurse when she was on Earth, and now contributed her skills to Saedo's hospital. She wore her brown hair in a neat bun on top of her head while placing Benjamin in a bassinet with a warm light underneath it.

"We'll keep an eye on him. He's beautiful." Isabella stroked his chubby cheek with her finger. "I didn't think they'd be this adorable. I imagined they'd—"

"Look like the horrid Ulkrins? Me too," Nina said.

After Isabella linked Nina's smart ring to a video that gave updates on Benjamin, she headed out to visit Amelia.

Nina took the glass elevator up to the second floor toward the adult wing of the hospital. When she found out that Zeycott and his brothers had successfully rescued Amelia, joy overflowed in Nina. Benjamin would have his mother by his side.

From what Nina was briefed on, Amelia had a long road

to recovery ahead. The damn Ulkrins did extensive and harmful experiments with all kinds of chemicals and devices to expedite the pregnancy and the baby's birth. Nina understood that normal human pregnancy was around nine months to ensure a healthy baby. And based on what she'd recently learned from the nurses in Saedo, alien pregnancy ranged from five to six months, depending on the species. Higher frequency allowed for healthier growth and faster cell division—all the science stuff that she didn't understand.

Despite that, the Ulkrins wanted an even faster growth. *Bastards.* Human bodies couldn't adjust that quickly without a destructive impact on the body and mind.

Nina spotted her sister Emma typing something on the virtual screen at the desk. With her nursing background, working at the Village Center Hospital had been the perfect fit. She worked part-time and used her time off to study the various alien anatomies so she could treat more patients. Also, she needed to catch up on her knowledge of high-tech equipment that wasn't available on Earth.

"How's Amelia doing?" Nina jerked a chin into the room where Amelia lay with eyes closed and a droid monitoring her vitals.

Emma tapped a button on her computer and sighed. "She's dehydrated, and her body's fighting to stay alive. She suffered an awful infection after giving birth that went untreated. The soldiers got her just in time. If she had stayed in that place for another day without care and medication, she would have died. Her will to survive allowed her to live this long. It's going to be awhile before she recovers, but she's strong."

"That could've been us, Emma."

"I know. We got lucky." Emma placed a hand on Nina's back and rubbed circles. "How are you doing? As your oldest sister, I should scold you for taking off after an Ulkrin. I can't believe you. What were you thinking?"

Nina wasn't in the mood to talk about it. Zeycott had reprimanded her—something that still irked her—and now her sister had the same reaction.

Was her action reckless? No, she didn't think it was. She had a reason. Yes, it had been dangerous, and she had been terrified, but if she hadn't gone after them, the consequences would have been worse. The Ulkrins could have cracked into the Silver Text and used that knowledge to hurt *all* of Saedo.

Besides, what was wrong with trying to save the man . . . the man she loved?

Her throat tightened as fatigue and emotions tangled into knots. She wasn't sure if she'd compose coherent sentences if she tried to explain to her sister now.

"I wasn't using my brain. I was using my heart, Emma." Nina dropped into the empty chair beside the desk. "Do you have anything to drink? I'm parched."

"Here." Emma offered a Saedo apple drink, which was a purple gradient drink with bits of sweetened jelly bits. Her sister plopped down in the chair beside Nina and stared at her.

"What?" Nina asked, sipping her drink.

"You're in love, aren't you? When did this happen? How did it happen? Why haven't you said anything? Does anyone know?" She crossed her arms. "Am *I* the last one to find out?"

Nina placed the metal can on the table beside her and scrubbed a hand down her face. She needed a shower and a bed. "Since when did you become my mother?" A headache throbbed behind her temples.

"Since Mom and Dad left you and your sisters to lil' ol' me. Now spill it, and I'll give you a tasty painkiller for your headache." She jabbed a finger into Nina's arm, which hurt a little. Her body needed sleep.

"You're evil." The headache pulsed as though agreeing with Nina.

"And you're not? My little sister is in love, and I—as the mother figure—need to know a few things. Does he love you? Did you see his mist?"

Nina released a sigh. "I'm not sure when or how it all started. I thought he was gorgeous, but the attraction intensified when we hung out. Yes, I've seen his mist. And no, I don't know if he loves me. I mean, I know he cares about me. But caring for someone isn't the same as loving them. You care for your patients, but you don't love them the way you do Raeko, right?" Nina opened her palm. "Now give me my painkillers before I turn into the evil sister you don't want to be related to."

Emma dropped a square pink and blue pill into Nina's palm. "These are new flavored painkillers. They taste like candies."

Nina took the pills and swallowed them down with a swig of the drink. She tossed the empty can into the trash receptacle and got up, preparing to go home and shower.

"I think you should ask him. Sometimes men are so oblivious to things." Emma offered Nina a one-armed hug.

"I will. But first I need to go home, shower, and get some sleep."

Emma made a face, sniffed, and grinned. "Oh, is that

you? I was wondering what that awful smell was. And you look horrible, by the way."

Nina rolled her eyes. "Thanks. You're a very *supportive* and *encouraging* sister."

"I try."

Nina called a ride service to pick her up and take her home. Too many things spun in her head as she waited for her driver. Her smart ring buzzed, and a message from Zeycott flashed.

How are you doing? Can I see you?

She wanted to say so many things, but she didn't know where to begin. She just wanted to be alone for tonight to gather herself.

I'm okay. Tired. Going to bed now. We can chat later.

That message should satisfy his concerns for now.

When Nina entered her apartment, she dropped into a heap of exhaustion on her couch. The White Mutaat crawled out from her pocket, and she bolted up.

"Ahh!" She pointed at it. "*You.* Stop trying to give me a heart attack."

It scurried down her leg, across her floor, and claimed a spot on her coffee table.

What the hell?

She'd meant to tell someone about the spider. It was odd that it didn't even make its presence known while she was at the hospital.

Nina eyed it. "Are you some kind of fantastical creature?"

It stared at her with its many eyes and made some weird noises. She didn't know if spiders made any noises, but she had never been interested in them to learn. In fact, she had stayed away from them as much as she could. But here she was *talking* to a freaking multi-legged giant bug in her apartment like it was her *pet*.

This was crazy!

Another thing she'd forgotten was the Silver Text tablet in her other pocket. When it looked undamaged, she blew out a sigh of relief. She'd meant to share it with Emma and Isabella, but too many things had crammed her mind.

She placed it inside an empty shoebox, put the lid on it, and moved it to the kitchen counter. Tomorrow, she'd visit Grandma Ova. Questions had to be answered.

But for tonight, a hot bath was all she needed to soothe her exhausted heart and sore muscles.

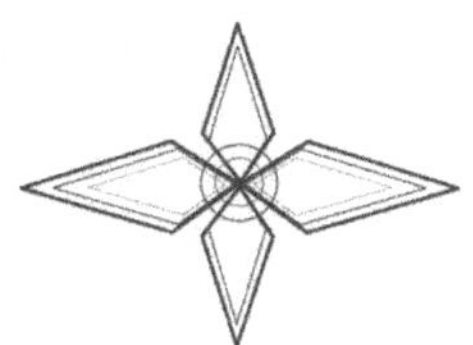

EIGHTEEN

Nina slept later than she had expected. She called in to work and requested some time off to recover. They all knew about the rescue mission that had occurred yesterday in the woods near the border of the Province of Finntoro.

She checked her smart ring and pouted when she didn't see any replies from Zeycott. She had needed time and space. Her message had been clear last night. So why was she irritated that he didn't reply?

He could have at least sent an "okay" or "see you later." *Anything.*

She could be "judgmental" too. She could scold him for his lack of judgment when accepting female clients with enormous chests who groveled over him. She could also remind him about how he should've taken better care of his health knowing his condition. Or that he should smile more. She could go on and on.

Just because she was stupidly in love with an oblivious green man—who had no right to have such a devastatingly beautiful face and body—didn't mean she'd lost her mind.

Did it?

The fact that she was sitting in bed analyzing showed that Nina had fallen too deeply for him. How the hell was she supposed to climb out of this emotional well?

She washed up, made herself presentable, and got dressed in a soft knit top and a pair of black Ingavex pants with metabolizing properties that toned the butt and thighs when she moved.

She retrieved the Silver Text from the box on the nightstand, and the weight surprised her. She didn't remember it being this heavy. Maybe her attention to detail had been off because of the desperate escape with Benjamin.

She patted the tablet. "I'm so glad you're safe."

"Thank you for protecting us."

Nina stopped in her tracks and glanced around her bedroom. She couldn't make out whether the gentle voice was male or female. No goosebumps or chills, which meant she had nothing to fear.

Despite that, caution had her scanning her bedroom and all the other rooms.

"Who are you? Where are you?" she asked, peeking in one room at a time.

"Ancestors of the land."

Surell, Zeycott's mom, had been one of them. Their conversation seemed like it had been ages ago. But this voice speaking to her now wasn't Surell.

"You saved Saedo from the evils of the Ulkrins. We're grateful for you and your sisters."

"You're welcome. Thank you for giving us a home when we needed it."

Saedo has been blessed with your presence.

Nina clasped her hands together and asked, "Can you tell me how I can save Zeycott? Surell said there's a cure in here for the osteomites disease."

"There's information woven into the wisdom of these pages, but you already know it. You have all the pieces—now connect them. The healing process is for you and Zeycott to discover. It is your journey. Both of yours."

Resigned, Nina pressed her lips into a tight line. "Yesterday, when I had you in my pocket, you didn't feel heavy like you do now. Why is that?"

Multiple voices laughed, but when spoken, they became one. *"Excellent perception. That's because we hid some data and made the tablet lightweight so the Ulkrins couldn't track it. Just as you 'forgot' about it, its energy was forgotten by the radars of Ulkrins."*

Nina's eyes widened when the White Mutaat hissed at her feet, and she jumped back. "Is this spider poisonous?"

"Don't be afraid. That's a rare White Mutaat. They're nearly extinct. He chose you because he resonates with your energy. Like a pet who wants to come home with its owner, it followed you."

Nina scrunched her face. When she thought of pets, a small dog or an adorable kitten popped into her mind, not an arachnid with too many eyes and legs.

The white spider crawled near her foot and tapped her toe with one of its legs. She withdrew her foot immediately. Geez, this was weird.

"We have a message to help you on your way. Bones are sacred because they last through many lifetimes. They tell a story of that individual. Your energy, your love, has transformed the evolution of bones all together. That is cosmic

magic. Turning poison into medicine is a blessing not only for Saedo, but for the Cosmos, including your Earth. Thank you, Nina, for your service."

The voice faded with an echo.

Nina didn't understand their message, but she knew who could. She took a plastic container with a handle. "Get in there, c'mon. We have somewhere to go," she told the White Mutaat.

It crawled out of the shoebox and into the smaller container with a tight lid. She got dressed and hopped into her personal rider, heading to Grandma Ova's.

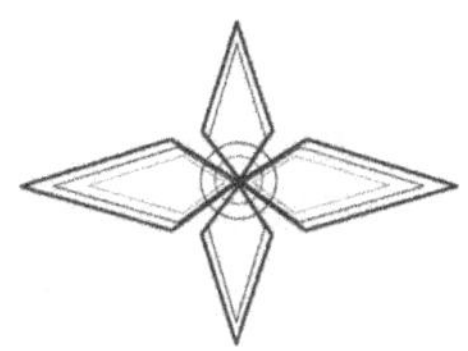

NINETEEN

As she drove, a message from her smart ring splashed onto the virtual screen.

How are you feeling? I need to see you.

Now he texted her.

Nina spoke her reply and sent it. *Better. Thank you. Heading to Grandma Ova now.*

The rest and time apart had served her well. Her brain could form coherent thoughts, and her heart was in a better shape today. She didn't feel depleted like yesterday.

Despite how Zeycott's words had hurt her, he had also saved her. *Twice.* She needed him to review the Silver Text with her. After all, the entire reason she went after the Ulkrins was for his safety. Like Emma said, maybe he was being an oblivious idiot and didn't understand the simple fact that a woman in love became an invincible force. Whether that invincibility was rational or irrational was an entirely different matter.

Nina asked her virtual screen to switch to Benjamin's

monitor. The screen showed him fully awake, babbling something while Isabella changed his diaper. A female doctor with orange hair and three eyes checked his vitals. His gray skin appeared lighter today, and his features had changed a bit too, looking more like his mom. Baby Benjamin cried, and Isabella swaddled him and hummed a lullaby that silenced him immediately. She'd always been good with children. If Nina started singing, the baby would have cried even louder.

Though Nina was safe now, concern for these villagers weighed on her. The soldiers didn't catch Commander Kruegen. He had disappeared along with a few of his creatures. She worried when the next attack would happen. She could feel it in the air. The anticipation prickled at her.

Nina arrived at Grandma Ova and her heart leaped at the sight of Zeycott's rider already parked in the lot beside the massive house. How had he gotten here so soon? Or had he been here already when he sent her the message?

She heard laughter coming from the back of the house. She grabbed her shoulder bag and the container with the White Mutaat and walked by the immense gardens. Vibrant butterflies with four wings and six wings fluttered past her. The flapping of wings created a singsong rhythm that stopped her in her steps. She listened to the relaxing melodies and made a mental note to consider it for background music for her yoga videos.

She didn't need to film any new videos for another week. She'd been so wrapped up in Zeycott's health and the Ulkrins that she hadn't even checked her channel. How did the viewers react to her yoga lessons? Did they love them? How many new subscribers had she acquired since posting the new videos? How many credits did she earn from the classes? She'd check later.

A delicious scent of something wafted her way, and her tummy growled. She hadn't eaten breakfast, and now it was close to noon. Time seemed to slip by too quickly these days.

Nina found Zeycott and Grandma Ova on the back deck. A swarm of butterflies hovered around, looking like floating ornaments. Zeycott wore an apron as he grilled something on a robotic griller she hadn't seen before.

She stood below the deck and watched him. Whatever conversation he was having with Grandma Ova brought a softness to his face. From her angle, he didn't look like someone suffering from a deadly disease. That just proved that you couldn't judge someone from looking at them. You could never fully know the extent of what others were going through.

With that thought, his words from yesterday echoed in her mind. What had gone through his mind when he said she lacked judgment? What had he been feeling? If the situation had been reversed, would she have reacted the same way?

Probably. Her stomach tightened.

Butterflies surrounded her suddenly, and Zeycott looked over and smiled. She shifted in her stance as nerves fluttered in her stomach like the colorful swarm around her. Why were they encircling her? She didn't smell, did she?

Zeycott made his way down the deck. "Afternoon." He placed a hand on each shoulder. "You look better."

Grandma Ova waved. "Hungry? Come on up. We're trying something new today."

"You look better too," Nina said.

"Oh? I thought I always look good to you."

She narrowed her eyes. "That depends on *someone's* mood."

"I see. I must have been some evil monster to you yesterday." He looked at her. "We'll discuss some things later, okay?"

Nina nodded, and her stomach made a vicious noise that had Zeycott and Grandma Ova laughing.

"There are many things to talk about today. But we must first feed our stomachs." Grandma Ova brushed some loose hair away from Nina's face. "How are you doing? I heard about your adventure." She leaned in and whispered, "It's worth it, isn't it?"

Nina met Grandma Ova's all-seeing eyes. This wise woman seemed to know everything. Or was Nina that obvious to read?

Nina glanced over at Zeycott, who was busy cleaning the robotic grill with the two red eyes that dimmed when he closed the lid.

"It was," Nina whispered back.

"Just take your time with him. Some men require extra explanation. Their brains work differently from the mighty female brain." She winked. "When you add love to the mix, it makes them even crazier." She emphasized with a tremble in her body that made Nina laugh.

"What's so funny?" Zeycott asked as he placed down a tray full of charred things.

A sealant covered his thumb. Was he injured during yesterday's battle?

"What happened to your finger?" Nina asked.

Grandma Ova smiled. "He insisted on helping me chop

up some herbs to marinate the hemaroots. It's from this hema-tiss plant." She reached over to a basket full of vegetables and herbs and pulled out a plant with oval-shaped leaves with purple edges. It had purple peapods, and the odd-shaped roots were yellow.

Nina examined a root closely. "It looks like a potato."

"Doesn't it? The hematiss plant replicates the taste and texture of blood. That means you can eat meat-flavored food without having to kill any animals. I have several recipes whenever you want to try."

The cutting-edge plants on this planet never ceased to amaze her. Nina returned the hemaroot to Grandma Ova and looked over at Zeycott, who hadn't said a word since she sat down. "How did you hurt your finger?"

Zeycott shrugged. "It's nothing."

"It was more than nothing." Grandma Ova waved a finger at him. "The cut will heal in a few hours. I gave him an extra healing balm with cooling sealant. He peeled the hemaroot with a regular knife and didn't use the special root peeler, which could have saved him time. I told him to leave it to me, but he *insisted* on doing it himself. He wanted to cook you something all on his own. I say he's a keeper."

Oh. Nina's heart twirled, and any irritation that had clung to her finally disappeared. "Thank you. I can't wait to dig in."

"He even dug up the roots himself." Grandma Ova used tongs to drop a hemaroot onto her white plate. "Try it. Let me know what you think."

Nina looked down at the hemaroot slices covered in spices and herbs and inhaled the appetizing scent. She poked it with her fork and brought one slice to her lips, biting into it. The spices burst in her mouth, taking on a juicy flavor.

"Wow! It tastes like chicken. I can't believe this is from a root. I'll need to stock up on these."

Zeycott shot up his arms in victory. "Yeah!"

Grandma Ova laughed. "I guess you passed your first time cooking a hemaroot with my recipe."

Nina offered him a warm smile. "Thank you for cooking. I appreciate it."

She didn't like this invisible wall between them. Had she been the one to put it up? She hadn't meant to, but now that it was up, she feared he wouldn't want it down. It had taken him a while to let her in and show her his emotions.

Did he regret any of it? Why did it seem like yesterday's minor annoyance had turned into something bigger? Was she overanalyzing again? He obviously still cared for her, otherwise he wouldn't have cut his finger cooking for her, right?

Nina gave her brain a rest so she could enjoy the hemaroots, which was her new favorite vegan dish.

For the next hour, everyone enjoyed a delicious lunch without discussing yesterday's event. No one asked questions that would have brought up important yet distasteful issues like the Ulkrins and their experiment on human females carrying their babies. Nina welcomed the respite. It was exactly what she needed. Good food and good company made her day.

When lunch was over, everyone settled around the table sipping the midori melon drink from the Saedo melon fruit. Nina took the Sacred Tablet out of her purse and placed it on the table.

"This is the reason I went after the Ulkrins." She glanced over at Zeycott, who sat beside her. "I woke up hearing voices, then I saw a translucent image fluctuating in front of me. I thought I had been dreaming until I saw Ulkrins and heard they had the Silver Text. They had taken it from a tattoo place." She turned and gripped his arm. "I totally forgot about that part. I think they went to your shop. We should check it later."

Zeycott nodded. "I'll send a message to Elleo to have her check it out."

Nina eyed him. "I wanted to yell for you, but they could hear me. A dry blade of grass crunched under my foot and made a sound. They heard it. I pitched a pebble at you, but you didn't budge."

"You should have found a bigger rock." Grandma winked, and Zeycott's lips curved a little.

"When the portal faded, I stepped through. I had no choice. I didn't want to lose sight of the tablet. I needed it . . ." She swallowed and chose careful words that wouldn't reveal her vulnerable heart. "Saedo needed it. I didn't know what Commander Kruegen would do with the information on the tablet, but I knew it wouldn't be good."

"Thank you, Nina." Grandma Ova held the tablet in her hands. "It would have been devastating to Saedo and all of Celeron."

"He had it hooked up to a machine that tried to extract its data, but I stopped it. I'm not sure how much info he got from it, if any."

"My brothers and I destroyed the underground tunnels, although a few Ulkrins escaped. Who knows what they took with them?"

"How long have those tunnels been there? It seemed established."

A muscle in Zeycott's jaw ticked. "You're right. They've been there at least six months, which means they've dug up the area way before that. Our radars missed it. We've underestimated the Ulkrins. I've alerted our allies, the Finntoros, because the tunnel extended over to their border as well. We'll need to do a thorough scan for any other underground posts."

Nina turned to Grandma Ova. "How was it possible that I could enter that portal? Why me?"

"The ancestors of the land wanted you to see it. You were resting in the pink grass, which can put your mind and body at ease. During the serene state of mind, magic occurs. You're able to connect to various worlds when your brain isn't cluttered. The Silver Text wanted you to know it was in the wrong hands, so it alerted you. Has it shown you anything on it?"

"No, not yet. I spoke to it, though."

"Spoke to it?" Zeycott asked.

"With my mind. It said something about bones. I see the bone symbolism all around me. My energy makes Zeycott's bones spark. And now the ancestors are talking about bones too. But I can't seem to connect the pieces together. What are they trying to tell me?"

"Perhaps I can help with that." Grandma Ova's eyes gleamed. "The body needs bones to produce bone marrow. Bone marrow is the location where blood cells are created: red blood cells, which carry oxygen around your body; white blood cells, which defend your body from diseases; and platelets, which clot blood when you have a cut. These are all vital for your body to function so you can live. It's basic knowledge, but underneath that generic data is a complicated system to *maintain* life."

Nina went on a hunch. "So . . . does that mean something is wrong with Zeycott's bone marrow?"

"But we've tested my bones and bone marrow before. No one could understand why the osteomites appeared or how to get rid of them."

"Maybe that's changed. We should get you tested tomorrow. We don't have time to waste," Nina said with conviction.

Zeycott's lips curved at her concern.

A rattling sound came from the container on the table. "I found this . . . thing while I was in the tunnel." She opened the lid to let the White Mutaat crawl out. "It kept following me around."

She recalled the spider had given her a direction when she came to the fork in the tunnel. If it hadn't been there, she might have been killed by the brown poisonous spider. She shivered, trying not to think about it. Plus, the White Mutaat destroyed the doorknob for her to escape with baby Benjamin.

The White Mutaat crawled around the table and came to sit in front of Zeycott, stared at him, and then returned to Nina.

"Isn't it a strange spider? I'm not a fan of spiders at all."

"I know. You assassinated the tiny one in your apartment," Zeycott reminded her.

The white spider made an odd sound, as though it understood.

Grandma Ova held out her hand, and the white spider crawled on it. "Hello there, White Mutaat."

"The ancestors said it's almost extinct."

"This is an extremely rare spider. It's not native to Saedo. There weren't that many of them to begin with, but there are fewer of them now."

The many eyes on the spider looked around, and Nina found herself not as frightened as she once had been. Had she adjusted to having it around her? Or was it because it had saved her from the Ulkrins?

She narrowed her eyes at it. "Are you a friend or a foe?"

It shot out a thread of silver silk that connected to a nearby plant. Then it began creating the most intricate and beautiful web that glistened in the sun. The design reminded her of a mandala. Then the mandala shifted to another unique design, then another, mesmerizing Nina.

"I think you got your answer," Zeycott said.

"You've been blessed to connect to the White Mutaat and have it accompany you. You don't understand how divine this is. Their silver liquid shapeshifts."

Nina clapped her hands together. "It can save Zeycott!"

"It can." Grandma Ova beamed.

"How?" Zeycott asked.

Grandma Ova let the White Mutaat crawl up her arm, across her shoulder, and down the other arm to sit on top of her palm. "The reason we can't obliterate the osteomites in your bones is because every medicine we've tried can't attack the virus. It shapeshifts inside your body, so it's hard for the defense system to 'recognize' it. The virus confuses the immune system." She gently tapped the spider's legs as though counting each one.

"I saw this little guy's liquids destroy another brown

spider that released a tar-like substance that also moves and shifts. But the silver liquids destroyed the tar."

"Nina, you don't understand how fortunate you've been. You also encountered one of the deadliest spiders on this planet, the Lycos Fera. Its tar could have seeped through your skin and killed you instantly. It's that potent."

Her skin tightened with goosebumps. Had she been that lucky? She recalled how close she was to that poisonous spider.

Zeycott placed a hand on her back, rubbing up and down. "You encountered both extremes of spiders, the worst and the best of these creatures."

"Poison and medicine," Grandma Ova added.

"The ancestors mentioned that too." The wheels in Nina's brain turned. "The osteomites is the poison. My energy is the medicine. This spider resonates with my energy, and now it's the key to turning the osteomites into medicine. If this remedy works, it's medicine for the Cosmos."

A warmth rushed through her like a confirmation.

"You connected the dots." Grandma Ova smiled.

Nina turned to Zeycott. "You're going to be okay."

"I'll be okay as long as you're safe." He pressed his lips into a thin line. "You risked your life for me. I'm grateful, but please don't do that again."

Grandma Ova rose from her chair. "I'm going to need some time to acquaint myself with our new friend. Hopefully, he'll let me extract his silver liquids. I'll set up an experiment to test it out before giving it to you. This is the breakthrough we needed, Zeycott."

For the first time, an inner light gleamed in his eyes and lit up his entire face, transforming what she had deemed as handsome to cosmically stunning. She didn't think she'd ever use that word to describe a man, but this man—*her man*—was exactly that.

"Do you need my help?" Zeycott asked.

"No, I'm all set. Thank you, though." Grandma Ova pointed to the excess leftovers. "Why don't you pack up the food and save it for later?"

"Then we can go check on your tattoo parlor," Nina said.

He nodded and looked at Grandma Ova. "We'll drop off the Silver Text at the Central Command Center for safe-keeping."

"That's a good idea. I think the tablet has accomplished connecting the two of you. The Copper Text would be happy to have its friend back."

Nina walked up to the White Mutaat on Grandma Ova's arm and touched its legs. That little gesture was a milestone in itself. She didn't even feel squeamish. "Be good, okay? We'll be back."

The White Mutaat hissed, and a teasing smile crossed Zeycott's face. "I think you have a new pet."

Of all the creatures she could have adopted on this vast planet, somehow a spider befriended her and transformed her aversion into a friendly fondness she still didn't quite understand.

"I think so too." Nina sorted the containers for Zeycott to pack up the food. "Would you help me take care of it?"

"You don't even have to ask." He brushed his hand over her cheek, a gesture she'd missed so much. She leaned into his touch.

"I'm sorry I scared you when I left. I couldn't let the Ulkrins steal the only thing that could save you."

"I know." He kissed her forehead, her cheek, and her lips. "And I'm sorry for being pissed at you. Yesterday I was mad, worried, and happy. I said words I didn't mean. Forgive me and I'll give you a gift."

She laughed. "What kind of apology comes with a bribe?"

The musky scent of him heated her body when he whispered, "The kind that promises fun, adventure, and . . . pleasure." His warm breath fanned her skin, sending a heated jolt to her core.

This man could elicit reactions from her body like no one else.

"You're forgiven." She jabbed a finger at his stomach. "Don't do that again. Don't underestimate my reasoning. There's always a reason behind my madness."

He tapped her nose with his finger. "I see that now, and I love your madness."

"I can't wait to drive you mad . . ." She trailed a finger down his abdomen and palmed his erection.

He gasped. "I need . . . to pack . . . this food . . . for you. It's . . . dinner."

She loved watching him grow weak for her. Because of her. "I don't need it. I already have what I want for dinner."

"You're so bad." He reached back and palmed her ass. "My kind of woman."

After they packed all the food into containers, Zeycott asked to see the Silver Text. Their hands touched while transferring the tablet, and energy zapped loudly. A bright light glowed from the center of the tablet, expanding out like a blooming flower. Zeycott carefully placed the Silver Text on the table. When the brightness on the brown Saedonite stone dimmed, silver text in handwritten script flowed across the glassy surface of the tablet.

Virtual pages appeared and flipped like a book, creating a rushing melody. Geometric symbols that shape-shifted flowed up vertically and then back down.

"I've seen these shapes. They're the air pockets in your bones and on the abstract design of the sculpture I have of you."

"You have a sculpture of me? When? Where?" His gaze bore into her. "Why?"

"Long story. I'll show you later. Right now, we need to focus on the Silver Text." She didn't want to miss any important data.

The secret codes, divine symbols, spells, remedies, and stories revealed from the hand-written text showed why the Ulkrins wanted the sacred texts. They could enhance their star race. They could use the knowledge to manipulate energy to hurt others.

After a few moments, the virtual pages turned a bright silver, then slowly faded back into the tablet. The light at the center dimmed, and she took that as a sign that the Silver Text's mission was now complete. The rest was up to Nina and Zeycott.

Nina shivered as she thought about how Commander Kruegen had come close to extracting the information. "The Ulkrins could take over all of Celeron if they get their hands on these texts and successfully retrieve the data."

Zeycott probably sensed the anxiety from her and placed a hand on her lower back. "But I heard no one can access their information if they don't want it revealed."

"Thank goodness for that. The sacred texts are intelligent because they're a combination of all your ancestors."

"And you kept it safe for us, Nina. Thank you."

She looked up at him. "I did it for you."

"And I'm forever grateful. Let's take this tablet to safety."

After securing the Silver Text in the Central Command Center, they headed toward his tattoo parlor. She prayed nothing was damaged by the Ulkrins, but she doubted they left his place unscathed.

TWENTY

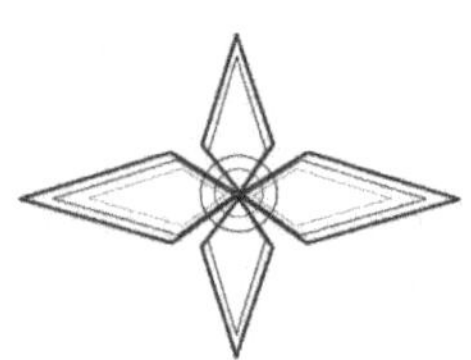

"Flekken!" Zeycott shoved away the wooden panel that blocked off the damaged wall, bookcases, and cabinets from view.

"Kenner and I did our best to cover it until you had time to see it," Elleo said, pointing to the giant hole in the wall. "I don't know what they were looking for here, but a tattoo parlor isn't the place for jewelry or artifacts. Dumbasses."

Zeycott and Nina exchanged a glance.

"Thanks for taking care of it for me, Elleo. You can take the rest of the day off. I'm closing the shop for a week for renovations. You'll get paid."

Elleo's eyes brightened. "Thanks! You're the best. I'm hanging with Kenner and his pals later today. I can relay the message to him."

"That would be great, but I'll send him a message too."

After Elleo left, Zeycott stood staring at the gaping hole in his wall.

"Do you need me to help you patch it up?" Nina asked. "I'm not very handy, but if you show me, I can learn."

He swung an arm around her shoulder. "Thanks, but I don't want you getting injured. I'm asking my brothers to come by when they're available. It'll be faster with them." He walked up to the wall and ran a hand over the unscathed area. "How did I not know about the Silver Text being here? How long was it hidden inside this wall?"

"The first time I was here, I saw a lot of silver sparks. Wasn't there a picture frame here or something?"

"Yes." He searched around and found a broken frame with a photo of him and his mother under a table. He picked it up, and his expression broke her heart. "We took this picture right before she passed."

"We'll frame it again. I think your mom was watching over you from the other side of the veil."

He turned the frame over and noticed an outline of the tablet's rectangular shape. "It was here all this time . . ."

"The Silver Text chose us," Nina said.

"Because it knew how potent we are together." His eyes intensified. "I think you should test that out."

Heat swirled around her core, but she wanted something first. "You told me to let you know when I'm ready for a tattoo. I'm ready now."

"What do you want?" He led her into his studio and gestured for her to sit on the chair while he prepped his equipment.

The idea came to her last night before she fell asleep. She wanted something to acknowledge their union. "I want a design that uses orange mist and silver sparks."

His brows knitted together. "Why?" In his sage-colored eyes, an emotional storm brewed, making them dark and dangerous.

His storm ignited the whirlwind in her—the hurricane of emotion that forced her to disregard her safety and go after the Ulkrins. She had been willing to sacrifice her life to ensure that he had a chance of survival. Seeing the same emotion in him released her.

"Because I love you." She hadn't meant to tell him so soon. She wanted to wait until things had settled. But right now, he needed to hear it. And she needed to give it to him.

He released a controlled sigh as sparks glittered in his irises. So bright, so beautiful; they hypnotized her.

"You've completely undone me, Nina."

She bit her bottom lip. "Do you have any art like that available?"

"No, but I'll sketch something." He kissed her tenderly, mimicking the calm before the storm. "I love you too," he said.

Somehow, she had gone from sitting on the tattoo chair to straddling his lap with no memory of it happening. He'd seduced her. He nibbled on her lips and licked along her jaw. "I've never said those words to anyone besides my mom, but that's a different love."

"I know," she muttered as he kissed down her neck, and heat bloomed all over her body.

"Where do you want the tattoo?" The guttural sound of his voice made her thighs clench.

"In two places . . . my shoulder . . . and my femur."

He paused, lifted his face, and eyed her with wonder. "Why the femur?"

Nina had done some research after seeing how he had tattoos on his bones. The femur was considered the strongest bone in the body. "The femur is where you rest your hands when you're sitting. It's where you hold your babies on your lap."

His hand brushed against her thigh. "Like this precious baby straddling me?"

She answered with a kiss to his cheek. "It symbolizes strength, power, regeneration, and support. These are all qualities I see in you, and how I see myself when I'm with you."

"I'd be honored to ink you." Zeycott opened a virtual screen on his wristband and began sketching a few abstractions for her.

For the next thirty minutes, Nina remained on his lap and watched him create a unique tattoo for her. There was a deep level of intimacy in being part of the creative process that symbolized them.

She spent the time to study his features, which she already knew from memory. Still, she absorbed the angles of his face as he concentrated on the screen. He hadn't shaved in the past few days, and the stubble added a different roughness to him. She skimmed her fingers along his cheek, jawline, and rested her hand on his chin. Her fingers found their way to his lips.

He snatched her fingers and nibbled on them. "You're distracting me."

"I'm not. I'm just admiring you."

"You can admire me later. I've got a surprise for you." His wolfish smile heated her straight to her core.

"Oh?" She arched an eyebrow.

"What do you think of this?" He expanded the screen for her review.

Nina pulled her attention away from his face to the

swirly design tinted orange. Silver sparkles glittered around it. Her body relaxed at the sight of perfection. She loved the simplicity of the waves that mimicked mist. The art was complexity wrapped in simplicity. Love was the ultimate force of miracles that transcended galaxies.

She placed two hands over her heart. "I love it. You knew exactly what I wanted."

"Thanks." Pride gleamed in his eyes. "Do you like these colors? What about the motion? This is what it'll look like if you choose the motion ink."

"That's impeccable. Does the motion ink work on bones too?" The various shades of orange flowed around the design while silver stars sparkled.

"Yes."

"Wow. Let's do it."

Zeycott saved the image he created to a file.

"What are those gold-leaf-looking designs? Are those tattoos as well?"

He nodded and placed a featherweight sheet of gold leaf in her hand. Its edge blew from her breath. "I can get metallic gold on my tat?"

"You can have whatever you want. This gold leaf is part of a new line of high-tech communication tattoos called DermaPrint using a specialized derma ink that I created. The prototype is in the approval process from the Saedo government. Once it's approved, I can sell it to the public."

"You developed it?"

His face brightened with pride. "I can be inventive when I feel like it."

She wrapped her arms around him. "I'm so proud of you.

Can you show me what it does? I want to know everything about your invention."

"The DermaPrint sits on the dermis layer of the skin. I've added touch sensor data vaults, wireless communication that links to smart devices, and microphones installed within the print. This way, you won't lose or damage your smart ring, wristband, smart necklace, and so on. The DermaPrint is also waterproof. You can pick any design. Choose a spot where the skin is exposed to sunlight to be recharged. My brothers, Tammo and Huelik, seem to love it. They didn't have any communication delays or errors with their smart devices."

With her mouth hanging open, Nina stared at the incredible invention. "I changed my mind. No mist on my shoulder now. I want a DermaPrint around my ring finger to replace the smart ring I currently have. Can you do that? I know it hasn't been approved yet—"

"I can ink you a ring. I'm not selling my services. It's a gift to you. Plus, the government doesn't need to know any of that." His expression turned serious. "Are you sure you want it on your ring finger?"

Nina didn't need to think about it. "I love you, so it makes sense that you ink your orange mist on my finger. Unless you don't want—"

"No one else is putting anything on your finger unless he wants to die." Zeycott took her hand in his, studying her ring finger. "I thought about getting matching ones with you, but I wasn't sure you'd be interested."

The velvety petals of her heart opened like a rose. "I'd love to have matching ones with you. This is like a starmate ring set."

"It is. We're already linked by the mist, but this is a beautiful token that we can wear in gratitude for what the Cosmos has given us."

She pressed her lips together, trying not to cry as emotions rose in her. Her stunning star-being wasn't just a soldier; he was a brilliant and thoughtful man.

"But I still want to keep the mist tattoo on my bone."

Nina removed the smart ring and tucked it into her purse. Zeycott sprayed a numbing agent on her ring finger. He used a small portable tattoo machine to make an outline of the mist. Next came the derma ink, which filled the outline. The procedure for the DermaPrint ring didn't take long, and it was painless.

"All done." He sprayed a healing lotion and protective sealant around it. "This will heal in a few hours."

"Thanks." She stared at her beautiful DermaPrint ring while he got started on her femur tat. Testing her gadget, she pulled up a virtual screen and said, "Look up."

When he did, she snapped a picture of him and grinned. "This is the first photo using my exceptional new smart tattoo. I love it so much!" She kissed it.

Zeycott's eyes crinkled. "It looks beautiful on you. I'll do mine after I finish the ink on your femur."

The bone tattoo on her thigh was a bit uncomfortable and required an extra numbing agent. She chose the motion ink for that because she wanted the mist to flow inside of her. Nothing should ever be stagnant. Movement was life, and this art gave her the meaning of life: her forever bond with Zeycott.

"I need to buy one of these portable x-ray devices for when I want to look at it," Nina said when he was done.

"Take this one." He pulled out a portable x-ray scanner from a drawer. "I have another one here."

"Are you sure? I can pay you for it." She waved the scanner over her thigh, admiring his work.

He pouted. "You're my starmate. You don't need to pay me. I do things for you because I want to. It makes me feel good when I see you smile."

She pursed her lips and teased, "Then I'm going to take advantage of you."

He swept a hand down his body. "This is yours for the taking."

Smiling, she scribbled her name on his chest with her index finger. "That's my signature on your body. I've marked you."

The devilish grin appeared again. "If you'd like to thank me, agree to my experiment. I think you'd love it."

If eyes could talk, he just told her she was in for something unforgettable. "Okay, I agree. What do you have planned?"

She got up from the chair, and to her surprise, her tattooed thigh wasn't sore at all. She didn't even bother to question how or why. The advancement in medicine and technology in Saedo was beyond her comprehension. She was about to turn off the x-ray machine when it glimpsed his sternum.

"Stop. Don't move." Her heart soared as she held the x-ray scanner to his chest. "When did you get this?" She stared at her name, inked on his sternum with orange mist flowing around it like a protective circle.

"Last night at home. I have a small studio there. I was worried about you and also relieved that you were safe. I wanted you to be part of me forever, etched in my life. Etched in my bones."

Any shield she had around her heart shattered with his confession. Nina placed her hand over his chest and felt the thrumming of his heartbeat. "My corra is yours. I hope you know that."

He grasped her hand. "I do. And mine is yours too."

He truly loved her. She embraced him, and the wish she had tossed out into the Universe sang in her ears.

I deserve a man who loves me and supports my sense of exploration.

Releasing him, she narrowed her eyes. "So what's this secret experiment you have planned for me?"

"It's not really an experiment per se. More like an 'exercise.' You know, the kind that makes you sweat, sets your corra racing, and has you screaming my name."

The twinkle in his eyes promised a sexual escapade she was dying to experience. "I'm ready to explore."

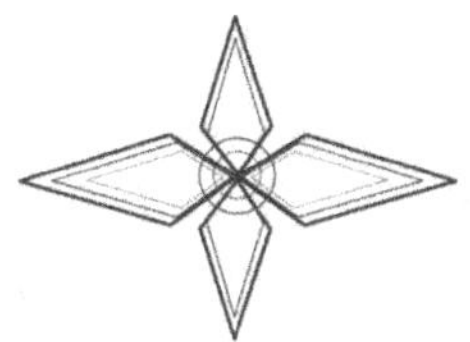

TWENTY-ONE

Zeycott retrieved a box from the corner of his studio and pulled out a small version of the robotic device that shot out energy bands like the ones in flying yoga class.

"No . . ."

"Yes . . ." he muttered. "We're having fun in my shop."

"What?" Nina glanced around at his tattoo studio and up at his ceiling. "There's not enough room. I don't want to damage your chairs or equipment."

Zeycott smirked. "There's another room over here." With the device in hand, he made his way down the hallway and into a bedroom.

"Oh." She gaped at the massive bedroom with an office in the corner. The ceiling wasn't as high as the one at the yoga studio, but it was high enough for them to have fun with the energy bands. His bed had warm brown sheets and pillows. The desk had several computers and other equipment she didn't recognize.

He walked up to her from behind, his chest emanated heat and his hard-on pressed against her buttocks. His hands slid up and cupped her breasts. She turned and the intensity in his eyes drew her in. She forgot the question she was going to ask him.

Desire erupted in her, fast and furious with lust gliding over her like lava. She wanted her hands on him, wanted his on hers. She gripped his top, yanked it off, and whipped it aside. The force almost sent the standing lamp to the floor.

A chuckle escaped him. "I thought I was the one in heat."

She didn't speak, couldn't. Need overwhelmed her to the point of speechlessness. With trembling hands, she tugged at his high-tech denim. He helped her, dropped everything, and kicked it aside.

Nina stared at his yummy body covered in slabs of honed muscles. She studied the broad shoulders, the taut abdomen that was its own masterpiece, and the grand green arousal that throbbed for her. As her fingers gently brushed his glorious length, she let out a throaty breath. He moaned, urging her to tease and taunt him. She wanted him to burn for her just as she burned for him.

Her fingers skimmed their way around his magnificent body, taking in every detail of him. She explored the terrain known as Zeycott, learning the firmness, crevices, and sensitive areas of his body. She ran her hand all over his well-defined back, squeezed his perfect ass, and admired the muscular thighs. To her, these were requirements for a warrior in the field and a warrior in bed.

Her thighs clenched as though she could hear his muscles whispering to her, promising her decadent things as long as she allowed them to tangle with hers. Her mouth watered, and she licked her lips. Zeycott yanked her body to him, and she yelped at the swift force.

"My turn." He crushed his mouth to hers, ravaged her until she was breathless. His lips kissed their way down her neck while his hands tore off her clothes. "My starmate, all bare and beautiful for me."

My starmate.

The words reverberated through her, sending a mad rush of adrenaline that fueled her system. The power of those words, the meaning and depth of them, seared into her blood, pumping her heart with a truth that brought tears to her eyes.

Nina wiped the tears away before he could see them, ask questions, and ruin this magical moment.

His hands stroked down her arms and body, and she shivered. He let out a low growling noise while he palmed her breasts. He captured a nipple and sent a jolt to her core. She moaned as a sexual tornado whirled through her, tossing all kinds of sensations around.

The lights in his bedroom dimmed, and the energetic bands surfaced from the robotic device he'd set up on the floor in the corner.

"Are you ready to have fun, Nina?" he asked in a throaty tone.

"Yes." She kept her eyes on the tattoos moving on his body, reacting to his arousal. The colors became more vibrant, and the motion flowed like water currents over his shoulder and arms.

The robotic device flew up to the center of the room and secured itself to the ceiling.

She yelped when the device shot out blue energy bands that wrapped around her waist and wrists, lifting her above the wooden floor of his room. Suspended in the air with her legs dangling, she felt like a sacrificial goddess.

When he licked his lips and shot her a starving look, hot liquid pooled at her center.

Zeycott walked up and smacked her butt playfully. "Tonight, we're creating our own sexual yoga. I've been thinking about those provocative yoga positions you introduced me to during the flying yoga class."

Excitement bubbled in her as she wondered what yoga form he wanted to try.

He walked around, scanning her body with heat radiating from his own nakedness. His face was eye-level to her ass. He made his way around to the front, stopped, and stared at her center. With his hands claiming each buttock, he pressed his face into her, inhaling her.

Fluids leaked out of her and dripped down her thighs.

"Flekken." His gaze flicked to the stream of wetness. "Mine."

He lifted her and placed her legs over his shoulders while the energy bands held her upper body in place. She felt both powerless and powerful. She was at his mercy, but she also held power over his need. Surrendering to him, she gasped when the velvet softness of his tongue licked up the juices adorning her thighs. Her body rocked when his mouth moved to her petals. His talented tongue deserved an award.

Sensations whipped through her body, blurring her vision. She moaned and writhed as he continued his feast. Her muscles tightened and clenched as she sensed a powerful orgasm brewing inside her.

"I love the way your body quivers for me," he said with a low growl.

The sound of his voice vibrated against her core, sending her soaring and screaming his name. Her body shuddered from an orgasm that ripped through her with the force of a fierce cyclone.

"Wow . . ." Nina breathed, trying to gather her brain cells that scattered during the beautiful explosion. She just wanted to touch him and tried to reach for him, but the energetic bands held her wrists.

Zeycott peered up at her with a wide grin. "I'm ready for the yoga sex pose."

"What . . . what . . . yoga position do you have in mind?" Nina could barely think, never mind compose complete sentences. She didn't think she'd have the energy for another potent orgasm.

His lips curved. "The scorpion pose. When I first saw you in that pose, I couldn't stop imagining me having you like that."

Her thighs clenched again, and it surprised her that her body could react so profoundly to him just after the tidal wave she'd experienced.

"Scorpion pose." Zeycott commanded the robotic device.

Several bands of energy shot down from above, assisting her naked body into the pose. A thrill of excitement zipped through her. He stood staring as several bands formed a platform for her hands and elbows to rest on, while more bands flipped her body backwards, making a C-shape with her spine and bent legs. The scorpion pose was like a curved version of a handstand where her legs were wide open. Maintaining this pose for a long duration would have been difficult, but with the energy bands carrying most of the weight, Nina was completely vulnerable to Zeycott's hunger.

"How come you don't have any bands on you?" she asked in a hoarse voice.

"Because I want easy access to your body from all angles. This is my signature on your body." Zeycott's hands and mouth roamed all over her, leaving fiery trails along the way.

As he ravaged her from all angles, his body sparked. Bright silver gleamed along his shoulders, chest, arms, thighs, and even face.

"Your bones—"

He covered her mouth with his and kissed her to oblivion. Her head spun from the probing of his tongue. She lost all train of thought except for how she wanted this kiss to never end.

She sensed his arms around her waist and neck as the energy bands released her body. He carried her to his bed and toppled over her. "I have so many poses I want to try with you, but I can't hold on much longer. I need you now." His erection throbbed against her center. "Should I use the Safe-Sex Spray?"

"No, I'm on the herbal pill."

"Great. This is the Zeycott pose, where you belong to me." He released a sound between a growl and a groan as he got on his knees and lifted her buttocks.

The tip of his arousal teased her entrance before sliding in. Sensation stormed through her as her muscles expanded to welcome his thickness. Sweat slicked his green skin, making him appear darker, more dangerous, like an emerald god conquering what he desired.

Pleasure rose and rose as he plunged deeper and deeper. Her thighs wrapped around him and tightened. She relished the feeling of him filling every inch of her. His eyes sparked with primordial need. *So many sparks.* She could only imagine what was happening inside his body—inside his bones—right now.

She had to ask. "Are you in any pain?"

"No, love." His chest heaved. "No pain. Only pleasure." His hips ground against hers, prodding. "You feel me?"

"Oh, God, yes." Loving the feel of him, her wild heart skipped, danced, and raced in her chest.

She fisted her fingers into the bedsheets as need coiled at her center like a tornado. "Zeycott!" A forceful orgasm tore through her, spiraling to every nerve ending in her body. Blood roared in her ears, and her body shuddered against his.

His entire body flexed, and the muscles on his face strained as he drove into her. Hard.

"Nina!" He roared out his pleasure like an untamed beast, spurting hotly into her. The pulse in his neck went erratic.

When he collapsed beside her, she pressed her face into the throbbing vein. "You were sparking everywhere."

He nuzzled her nose with his. "I wanted you so bad. I felt it in my bones." He drew her closer. "My yoga queen. Yoga sex is the best. This should be our daily ritual." He got up, went to the bathroom, washed up, and returned with a towel for her to clean up.

They cuddled for a moment. Then she looked up at him, fluttering her eyelashes. "Hi."

He arched an eyebrow. "I don't know if I like that mischievous look on you."

She bolted out of bed and dragged him with her. "We're not done yet. Since I'm your yoga queen, you've got to be my yoga king. *Prove it.* I want you in the tree pose, *right now.*"

Curiosity tickled her. Could he balance on one leg while

she had her way with him? How long could he maintain that pose?

Amusement gleamed in his eyes. "As you wish."

He stood like the proud warrior she had come to love, his erection became an attractive limb on its own. He shifted his weight onto his right foot while lifting his left foot and bringing the sole to rest on his thigh. His hands came together in a prayer mudra at his chest, and heat flashed in his eyes.

"I pray for lots and lots of orgasms."

She laughed.

Then he pointed to the floor. "Get on your knees for the king."

Nina did, pleasuring her king until he rewarded her with a new Zeycott pose that she was already eager to practice over and over again.

TWENTY-TWO

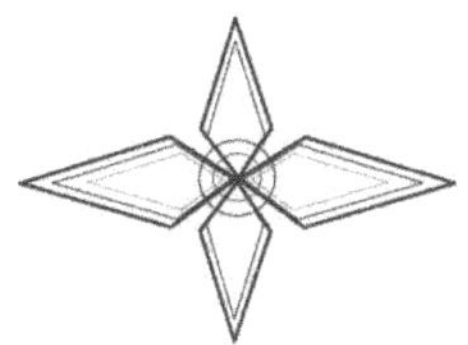

"Wow." Zeycott stared at the stone bust of himself. "It's stunning. It looks *just* like me."

She laughed. "You're *so* modest."

He ran his fingers over the geometric pattern on the side of his face. "It's truly amazing that you created this before we even found the Silver Text. It's like you tapped into another dimension and connected with the energy before it became reality."

Nina nodded thoughtfully. "It felt like a trance. I don't recall carving your face or the patterns. Grandma Ova said that my heart—my corra—guided me."

"You connected to me before you even realized how fated we were. I think you should display this in the living room. I don't want this handsome sculpture inside a dark closet."

"I was embarrassed then. I didn't want anyone to know I had a crush on you."

"And now?"

"Now I don't care." She placed the bust at the center of

the mantel for all to see. "Maybe I'll include it in the background of my yoga videos."

"Go right ahead. You can show me off to the galaxy. I can make a guest appearance too. This way, I can make sure the males know that you're with *me*."

For the next couple of days, Nina helped Zeycott make repairs at Versatile Ink. "Help" meant she walked around watching him and his brothers take down walls, put new ones up, paint, and rebuild the wood framing and so on.

"Are you sure I can't do anything?" Nina asked Zeycott when he walked past her. She sat on a chair inside his studio, editing her yoga videos.

He dropped a kiss on the crown of her head. "You're helping me by being here. I like looking at you while I'm working."

His brother, Huelik, who had lime green eyes and short brown hair, ambled by with a drill and teased, "*I like looking at you*, Tammo."

Tammo's teal eyes crinkled as he ran a hand over his bald head and flexed a bulky bicep. "*Am I 'helping' you by being here?*"

Zeycott strode out of the studio. "Assholes. Get back to work if you want to be fed."

A roar of laughter erupted amongst the green men. Men who have made her life in Saedo worthwhile, especially the annoyed man with hands on his hips directing his friends to finish up what they came to do. With their help, Zeycott could reopen his shop in just a few days.

She loved the dynamics between the soldiers of Saedo. They were the elite police force of the province. Besides working with Chief Mozar on government business, most of them had other occupations and interests.

Maeson walked up and slung an arm around Zeycott's shoulder. "We can badger them when they fall in love."

"You can wait a lifetime for that. I like my bachelorhood!" Tammo shouted.

Shaking his head, Macson slapped Zeycott's shoulder. "They know nothing."

While Zeycott and his brothers renovated the damages, Nina started a new collection for her video channel. After spending several nights with Zeycott experiencing various yoga sex poses, she realized that yoga could be implemented in the bedroom scene beautifully. She started jotting down ideas for basic yoga sex poses that were safe and fun for couples who wanted to explore. She'd be using animation for the demonstration and making the classes available for purchase. Maybe her yoga would help bring couples closer together.

Nina's phone buzzed with a message from Emma. *Amelia asked if she could see you. She's doing well.*

Great! I'll stop by later today.

Nina had already planned on visiting Amelia and Benjamin.

TWENTY-THREE

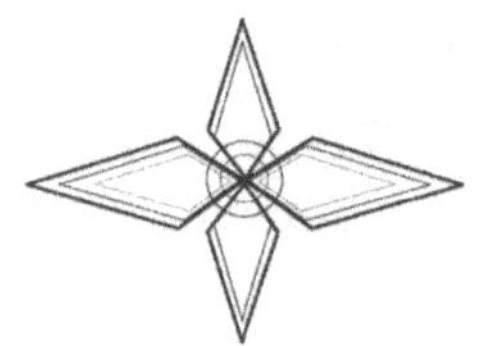

Nina and Zeycott made their way through the crowds wandering around the main lobby of the hospital. Some kind of intergalactic conference was taking place in the three conference rooms near the main area.

Zeycott held Nina's hand as they weaved their way through the groups of star-beings in suits and wearing white and gray overcoats. Nina accidentally bumped into a bulky star-being wearing a gray overcoat and a mask that covered most of his face.

"Sorry," she said, but he didn't hear her as he rushed off with another male toward the surgical area.

When they arrived at Amelia's room, they found her singing to her baby. Tucked in her arms, Benjamin looked up at her with loving eyes and babbled something. Nina held Zeycott back before he could open the door. They stood by the window to give Amelia and her baby some privacy.

"We can wait out here for a bit. It's their bonding time," Nina said.

"She looks so peaceful and happy." Zeycott interlaced his fingers with hers. A gesture she was coming to expect and love from him. "You saved her. You gave her this chance to be with her baby and watch him grow."

The moment tugged at Nina's heart as tears blurred her eyes and slid down her face. Zeycott brushed them off with his thumb.

"No one's going to hurt Amelia and Benjamin again."

Amelia walked around the room singing, smiling, and looking at peace. Compared to the day Nina met her, Amelia's hollowed cheeks had filled in, and her face brightened with color and hope. She walked by the window, glanced up, met Nina's eyes, beamed, and waved them in.

Nina smiled. "I hope we're not interrupting."

"Of course not. Isn't he beautiful?" Amelia shifted her body so they could see Benjamin.

"Oh, my! Look at those chubby thighs." Nina couldn't resist a gentle squeeze. "How are you doing?" she asked Amelia.

"Wonderful. Thanks to you." Amelia laughed when Benjamin babbled and reached up with his tiny fingers to touch her face.

"I think he's talking to you." Nina patted his patch of dark hair.

"He's saying he loves me. Isn't that right, my little pumpkin?" She turned to face Nina. "And that he's thankful to you." She turned to Zeycott. "And you and your brothers."

"You're welcome. Our responsibility is to protect the innocent and those in need."

Nina placed a hand on Zeycott's arm. "Zeycott and his

brothers saved me and my sisters too. We now live here as permanent residents."

"That's very kind of the community." She kissed baby Benjamin on his forehead. No longer looking harried and sick, her beauty rose to the surface. "Would you like to hold him?"

"I'd love to." Nina held Benjamin and noticed his weight had increased since she last picked him up. His face had transformed with two plump cheeks that added character to his personality. The birthmark on his forehead now had a gray texture. "He has such a cute birthmark here."

Amelia's expression softened. "I thought so too."

Zeycott peeked at the textured birthmark.

"Wanna hold him?" Nina asked.

"Umm . . ." He hesitated a moment, but then baby Benjamin looked at him, smiled, and babbled like he knew Zeycott.

"I swear, the power of cuteness never fails," Nina said and transferred the baby over to Zeycott. "You can sit down so you're more comfortable."

Nina and Amelia exchanged a smile at the awkward way Zeycott carried the baby.

He dropped into the armchair beside the bed, and her heart melted at his tenderness with the baby. Zeycott babbled, mimicking Benjamin's language.

Benjamin scrunched his face and his body shivered, then he smiled. Zeycott glanced up at Nina with confusion.

"You just got peed or pooped on," Nina said with a laugh.

"Oh . . ." Zeycott and Benjamin stared at each other.

"Don't worry, he's wearing a diaper," Amelia said.

Nina turned to Amelia. "Emma mentioned you wanted to see me. Do you need something? Are you still in pain?"

"I'm feeling somewhat better. It's mostly discomfort now, and my body's adjusting to medication well. The doctors here are amazing. I never imagined I'd be on another planet, having a baby, being cared for by aliens . . . No one truly knows how their life could change in an instant." She sighed and looked over at Zeycott, who was letting Benjamin hold his long finger. "The star-beings here are so different from the other ones I've met."

A chill snaked down Nina's body at the thought of the Ulkrins. How many more humans had been captured by them? Would the soldiers of Saedo be able to obliterate these monsters?

"Not all star-beings are bad. Just like humans, there are evil people too," Nina said.

Amelia sat down on a chair beside Nina and clasped her hands together. "I'd like to ask for your opinion . . . your help. I'd like to . . . stay here. You know, start over. Do you think they'll let me?"

Zeycott heard her and replied, "We'd love to have you. I believe the citizens of Saedo wouldn't mind having another lovely human female around."

Amelia's eyes glistened with tears. "Thank you. I don't know what to say."

"Just rest up so you can take care of your son. Take it one day at a time."

Baby Benjamin fussed, and Zeycott got up from the armchair and gave him back to his mom. "I'll get the documents ready for you. When you're up to it, you can go down to Central Command Center and sign them. We can help you find an apartment and get you situated."

Amelia shed more tears, but she smiled. "Thank you so much."

Nina looked at Amelia's wrist and neck but didn't see any smart wristband or necklace. "I'll get you a smart bracelet so you can contact me if you ever need anything. You can call or send me messages. You can also watch videos on the virtual screen when Benjamin is keeping you up at night."

Zeycott pulled up a virtual screen using his wristband. "I'll take care of the smart bracelet. There are a few extra ones at home. I can order a temporary one for you now. The drone will deliver it in a few hours."

"Thank you!" Amelia said.

Nina patted his cheek and whispered, "You're so efficient, my yoga king."

He narrowed his eyes at her, but she saw the smirk on his face before it disappeared.

Amelia placed Benjamin in his crib. "The doctor said I'm not well enough to breastfeed yet. They gave me milk for Benjamin." She gestured to the bottles on the cart next to her bed.

"That's fantastic. We'll let you feed him and get some rest. I'll stop by another time. I meant what I said earlier. Contact me if you need anything, even if you just want to talk. I know what it's like to be scared and excited to start a new life. I had my sisters to share those feelings with, but you don't. Consider me as a friend."

"I'd like that very much, Nina."

"We'll be back later to check on you. You can also reach

out to my sisters Emma and Isabella. They'd help you without hesitation."

As they left the room, Zeycott's wristband glowed with a call, and he pulled up a screen.

Grandma Ova waved at him and Nina. "Are you available tomorrow? I've made excellent progress. I'm ready to start your remedy."

Excitement burst in Nina, and she jumped onto him, giving the biggest hug she'd ever given anyone. Her legs wrapped around him like a spider monkey. Star-beings in the main lobby stopped what they were doing and glanced her way. Some smiled, some snickered, and some blushed.

Nina didn't care how she looked with Zeycott's hands on her bum. Zeycott was going to be cured of an illness that had plagued him, the one that had taken his mother's life. If this remedy worked, it was a gift to Zeycott in so many ways. Not only would it heal his body and heart, it would also heal his soul. The shattered parts of him would mend, and that was all Nina had hoped for.

"You need to go to bed early, so you can be well-rested for tomorrow's treatment." Nina untangled from his arms, hopping down to the ground.

He checked his wristband and made a face. "It's early. I've never gone to bed at this hour. Plus, I didn't hear Grandma Ova giving me any special instructions."

"She probably thought you already knew what to do before a critical treatment. It's common sense."

Zeycott laughed. "Since when did you become Dr. Nina?"

"Since I started sleeping with a patient who needs extra tender, loving care."

His laugh echoed as they exited the hospital and stepped outside. "Well, if I'm going to bed early, then I'll definitely need a lot of tender, loving care to help ease into sleep."

She slid an arm around his waist and grinned. "Great minds think alike. Any yoga pose you have in mind?"

"I have plenty." He smirked, and his eyes danced with wildfire.

For the first time in forever, she couldn't wait to go to bed early.

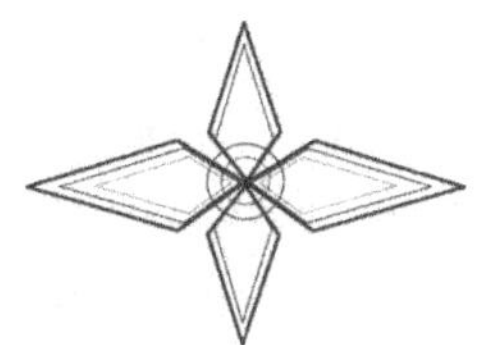

TWENTY-FOUR

"Was it difficult to extract the silver liquids from the White Mutaat?" Nina asked, staring at the glass condominium Grandma Ova had gotten for the spider.

The spider paradise was the size of her desk, made of all glass with small mesh sections in various places. He crawled around the terrain full of rocks and logs with enough crevices to play hide-and-seek and enough open space to chill.

"He was very cooperative. I fed him enough delicious food to entice him to provide me with more silver liquids. He's very intelligent. I just had to find the most effective way to communicate with him. He loves my pink grass jelly. Who knew? We're good friends now." She tapped the glass tank, and the spider crawled out from behind a log.

Nina placed her hand on the glass panel. The spider hissed and threw out a geometric web of silver threads.

"But he doesn't like me as much as he likes you. Look at that web!" Grandma Ova gestured to the mandala web on the glass.

"That's some intricate web. I'm jealous." Zeycott pouted,

studying the spider that stared back at him. "You behave yourself. She's mine."

"It took me two days to mix the silver liquids to create an effective serum. I tested it on an infected bone I retrieved from the hospital's archive room. They have a collection of specimens used for ethical experimental purposes. The family of the deceased donated them." Grandma Ova pointed to the three bones on the metal tray. "I had to adjust the serum with some herbal ingredients to dilute the potency of the silver liquid. It's powerful, and I needed something to help the bone marrow adjust to the potency and not bring it to shock. I can always give Zeycott more as his body adjusts to the serum."

"You should've asked us to stop by sooner to help you." Zeycott picked up the experimental bone labeled "success" and examined it. Silver had filled in the cracked area on the bone.

"You had other things to do." Grandma Ova waved a hand. "I like to work in peace." She gestured to the bed. "Situate yourself. Lie down so your body is in a relaxed state."

"Are you nervous?" Nina asked, rubbing Zeycott's back as he sat on the edge of the bed.

"A little." He shrugged and stared at the monitor floating in front of him.

Zeycott had borrowed an x-ray drone from the Central Command Center that would scan his body and display its reaction to the silver liquids. The portable device from Grandma Ova had lacked some of the features of the more powerful drone.

She cupped his face with both hands. "I'll be here. Think of this as a new beginning."

Nodding, he smiled. "I never imagined I could be cured. But here I am, sitting on the edge of it."

Zeycott lowered onto his back, and Grandma Ova held up a syringe with a tiny needle that squirted out a drop of silver. "Ready?"

Zeycott nodded, and she inserted the needle into the vein in his arm. Silver liquids entered his body, and the x-ray drone scanned him from top to bottom.

"That's amazing how I can see your veins and arteries sparking alive without the drone." Her eyes stayed on the serum as it moved around to every part of him.

Zeycott's gaze remained on the monitor as the x-ray scanner displayed the fine details of the process taking place. She could see the shape of the blood cells and the virus.

Nina gasped at the battle from within. Osteomites appeared like odd-shaped organisms with tiny filaments which looked like legs. They nibbled away at Zeycott's bone marrow by destroying his red blood cells, white blood cells, and platelets. She never thought she'd remember this much about biology, but seeing this incredible process in action helped her see the miraculous body and how it could defend itself.

When his bones flashed a spark, she turned to him. "Was that painful? That was like a lightning bolt of illumination."

"No. I think, with you beside me, my body is responding to your energy. It's stronger and fighting harder," he said.

Grandma Ova smiled. "You're right. The flash is your immune system reacting to the osteomites. Now watch the silver liquids as they surround the mutable mites that are shapeshifting faster than before. See how their filaments are multiplying? They're trying to confuse your immune system."

Nina compared the identifying process to mugshots of criminals, where the faces kept changing, making it hard to locate the one you had in mind. It was like a guessing game.

The silver liquids shapeshifted and encircled the virus, weakening it. Then the silver liquids subdued the virus, leaving the immobile mite for his body's natural defense to take over.

Orange mist with silver sparks appeared and flowed around him like a blanket of fog.

Zeycott's eyelids drooped, but he strained to keep them up. "Why am I so drowsy? Did you add something to the serum?"

"No." Grandma Ova placed a hand on his forehead. "I think your body is telling you to let go. Rest. Let it do its thing. Your brain is too active right now."

Zeycott let out a snore before he could reply. Nina spent the next twenty minutes watching the silver liquids obliterate the osteomites. After they did, the silver liquids merged with the blood cells. His entire body sparked like a million stars. When everything dimmed, his bone marrow appeared strong and clear of the disease. Even the "holes" within the spongy area of his bones appeared smaller, more natural.

Nina turned to Grandma Ova. "It's really repairing him." She watched the phenomenon unfold, and an idea popped into her mind. "With this discovery, we can cure all bone diseases. You have no idea what this could do for humans on Earth. It could save so many lives. We could obliterate osteoporosis forever. People wouldn't break a limb so easily."

"Yes, the White Mutaat is a rare creature that came to

you. It *chose* you. I'm going to continue working with it. Do you mind if I keep it here for a while? I'd like to acquaint myself with it better. Maybe it has other qualities we haven't discovered yet. Saedo is advanced compared to Earth, but there are other planets with higher frequencies that are even more advanced than us. I don't know everything, and this is an opportunity for more knowledge."

Nina couldn't imagine being more advanced than what she already witnessed in Saedo. But the Cosmos was a vast place, and she was just living in a province on one planet.

She tapped on the glass condominium and looked at the spider. "Please keep him as long as you need. It'll give me time to prepare my home for him. I never thought my first pet would be a giant spider. But then again, I never thought I'd live amongst star-beings either. Living here has taught me so much about myself." She shifted to Zeycott, who looked so peaceful on the bed. "What used to scare me has, in turn, saved me and the man I love. Fear is an interesting thing."

"It is. Most things we need are coated in fear. It takes courage to scrape the fear off. Like anything, it's a learning process, and sometimes it requires a purpose—a reason for you to initiate the desire to scrape it off. Your purpose was to save Zeycott."

Nina couldn't agree more. "You said that the Silver Text requires a sacrifice in order to receive its wisdom. I think you're right. I sacrificed my fear of the Ulkrins to go after the tablet. I had to dig for the courage to do what was right."

"You also sacrificed your life. You could've easily died." Grandma Ova patted Nina's back. "He'll be out for a few hours. Let him sleep. I have something to show you. Come with me."

Nina followed Grandma Ova out into her garden that thrived with life, vibrant colors, sweet scents, and gorgeous birds and butterflies. The two suns shone brightly in the sky. She wouldn't mind having a smaller version of this garden in her backyard when she could afford a bigger place to live. Her current apartment had little space for much.

They made their way through the garden toward the pink grass field, and her body tingled from the aroma. Another aromatic scent she didn't recognize stirred in the air. "What's that fragrance?"

Grandma Ova stopped by a section along the trail where orange flowers bloomed. They looked familiar to Nina, but she couldn't seem to place them.

"The scent is from these blessiums." Grandma Ova bent down and sniffed at a stunning orange flower in full bloom. "I've never encountered a blessium with such powerful aroma."

Nina's heart pitter-pattered as the realization hit her. She recalled her sister's blessiums, each color representing the mist of their significant other. "Is that . . ."

"The flower that you and Zeycott inspired to grow and bloom. The energy is unique this time. With every new relationship that develops, the energy in Saedo is stronger. The abundance of blessiums is proof of that. Your sisters' flowers didn't give off an aroma, or at least I don't recall them mentioning it."

"Maybe they're giving off the scent now."

"Could be. Energy changes, and perhaps these blessiums are responding to that."

Nina would contact her sisters to inquire later. Right now, the cluster of orange blessiums decorating the trail astounded her. Her sisters had spoken about one or two blessiums growing after they fell in love, but Nina was staring at fifty or more, each one a varied shade of orange. No wonder the fragrance was strong. There were so many of them in bloom.

"When did you notice them growing here?" Nina walked up to each one, smiling at them.

"The other day. I noticed the unfamiliar scent when I was working in my garden, so I went to check." Grandma Ova continued down the trail and came to the open space where Nina and Zeycott had slept that night. Another bunch of orange blessiums covered the ground. She plucked one from the cluster. "I think it's time to experiment with these blessiums. I wanted to before, but they didn't flourish in abundance like this. And I didn't want to risk killing the only flower your sisters had."

"Let me know if you uncover something interesting." Nina tapped her DermaPrint ring and a virtual camera appeared. She snapped some images and took a couple of videos.

What would Zeycott think of this? Had he seen the blessiums of her sisters?

Instead of calling or messaging her sisters, Nina made a trip to Sasha's house, which wasn't far from Grandma Ova's. She wanted to see Sasha's blessium herself.

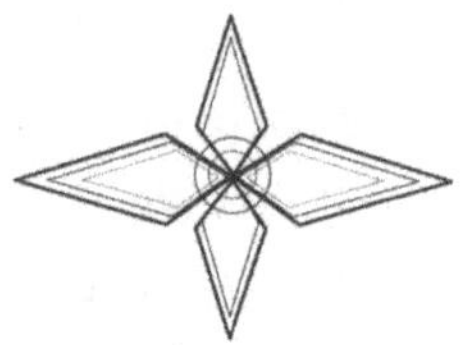

TWENTY-FIVE

To Nina's delight, all of her sisters arrived at Sasha's house except for Emma and Isabella, who were stuck working at the hospital.

"Show me the blessiums." Vanessa tied her red hair into a ponytail and tugged at Nina's arm. "I've been feeling a lot of dark energy lately."

Vanessa's admission worried Nina. Vanessa could sense things better than any other sibling. Nina pulled up the screen from her DermaPrint ring.

"What is that? Where's your other smart ring?" Sasha set down the brown mug of coffee that matched her long wavy hair and yanked Nina's hand for a closer look. She rubbed her finger over the inked ring. "It's flat. So cool. Where did you get it?"

Nina had a feeling Zeycott's prototype would be a big hit with her siblings. "It's one of Zeycott's tattoos. You can get any smart art tattooed on your body with state-of-the-art ink. And it links to your regular smart devices in case you need to access older data."

Inga examined Nina's finger. "I want one." She'd added more golden highlights to her light brown hair, which made her even more gorgeous.

"Me too," Rita exclaimed, twirling a strand of brown hair around her finger.

Nina had planned on discussing blessiums, not tattoos. But seeing how excited her sisters were, she couldn't help becoming Zeycott's publicist.

"It's still in prototype mode, but I'll ask him if he can start offering them to you before the public."

"We'd promote the heck out of it for him," Inga said. "I have another fashion show coming up in a couple of months. I'd be sure to show off my smart art. I'm not sure what I want, though. Maybe Osayik can give me some ideas."

"So, Nina... have you slept with Zeycott?" Sasha wiggled her eyebrows.

The house went quiet. Her sisters stared at her and each wore a grin that heated her face.

"Jeez. I didn't come here to talk about my sex life."

"Well, then let's start." Sasha laughed. "You don't need to go into details. How was it?"

Oh my God. Nina had never spoken to her sisters about her intimacy. Why were they suddenly curious now?

Nina narrowed her eyes. "It was mind-blowing. Unforgettable. Inspiring. How were *yours*?" She looked from one sister to the other.

"Same." They all burst into laughter.

"Okay, I'm ready to see your blessiums now," Rita said.

Nina opened a file on her virtual screen and played the video.

"Wow. Look at all of them." Inga placed a hand to her heart. "I've gotten a few extra blooms, but yours is a garden!"

"Between all of us, we've got a lot of colors covered. Emma's yellow, Sasha's blue, Inga's red, Vanessa's purple, Rita's teal, and Nina's orange."

"There's no doubt Isabella is the final sister, but what color would hers be?" Rita sipped a blue bubble tea that Sasha made with pink grass jelly bits she probably got from Grandma Ova.

"She needs to fall in love first." Vanessa nibbled on pastries she brought from her restaurant, Trust Your Gut. "She could fall for any of the soldiers."

"Do your flowers give off a fragrance?" Nina asked.

"Now that you mention it, I thought I smelled something the other day, but I dismissed it. It was faint, nothing too obvious," Sasha said, looking perplexed. "It didn't produce any scent when it first bloomed, though."

All the sisters confirmed their blessiums gave off a fragrance.

"Have you noticed anything different with your flowers?" Vanessa asked. "My purple flower has black spots on it. They come and go though. There's something going on with the purple mist too. The other day, I saw a black stream of mist around the purple."

Nina didn't notice any darkness around the orange flowers or the mist.

"You know what?" Inga held up a finger. "My flowers have some dark spots too. They disappeared later, so I ignored them. I haven't seen anything out of the ordinary with Osayik's red mist, though. But I've been having a lot of nightmares just this past week, and that's abnormal."

"I dismissed the dark spots on mine too. This is very strange," Rita said.

"I'll be right back." Sasha rushed out the back door.

Vanessa placed a hand on her stomach. "I've been feeling a powerful tug of war between the dark and light."

"Like Grandma Ova said, we're connected to Saedo," Nina said. "Maybe as our energies grow stronger, so does the dark. It's escalating to fight us."

"I think you're right." Rita sipped her drink.

Sasha returned from her yard and pulled up a virtual screen. "Check out my blue blessium."

The video showed dark spots shifting on the blue petals like moving shadows. The blue color was battling the black. The image reminded Nina of the fight between the silver liquid and the shapeshifting virus. Nina was looking at the battle between good and evil play out in nature.

Vanessa rubbed her stomach and inhaled a breath. "We'll have to pay more attention to these flowers and the mists, see if there are any other strange happenings. They're guiding us."

"And we're the key to helping Saedo," Nina added. "We'll have to update Emma soon."

All the sisters nodded.

"It's a miracle that none of the petals have fallen off either. I mean, I'm getting two new buds. See?" Sasha swiped the screen to show an image with her five flower buds.

"There's so much lore in Saedo," Rita said. "Each flower represents a color on the Love Spectrum—a cosmic frequency that nourishes the land and everything around it."

Nina added, "Grandma Ova said the energy is stronger each time new lovers discover each other."

Rita stared at the table, thinking. "I remember my conversation with the ancestors of Saedo. The Copper Text is the top layer in the Love Spectrum. The Copper Text represents smoke and mist—fire and water. They are symbols of flexible perception and the ability to enter different realms of existences and beliefs."

"They're polarities," Vanessa said. "Opposites. But when they resonate in perfect harmony, magic happens."

Rita gestured a hand to Nina. "You and Zeycott uncovered the Silver Text tablet, which is the middle layer of this spectrum. What's the symbolism here?"

Nina knew the answer in her bones, pun intended. "Bones."

"Bones?" Inga arched her perfect eyebrow.

Nina shared how Zeycott had reacted whenever he saw her. The pain on his face had stomped her heart too many times, and yet she still couldn't resist her attraction to him. But everything turned out to be a process—a plan—carefully orchestrated by the Universe. She even showed them a clip of his bone spark.

"I didn't think that was even possible." Inga stared at it in awe.

Rita leaned into the table and tented her fingers, thinking. "Hmm . . . smoke and mist. Now bones."

"Bones are like heirlooms we leave to the soil. Zeycott developed this device where you can get tattoos on your bones using laser beams. You can add art, words, or whatever you want. So when you pass, you leave that part of you—*your story*—to the land, to your family."

"That's morbid . . . and beautiful," Sasha said.

"I think it's fitting that the Silver Text represents the

middle layer of the Love Spectrum," Nina said, trying to organize the thoughts circling in her mind. "Bones are the support structure of the body. The bone marrow is essential to life itself. That's the center—the home—where blood cells are produced. Symbolically, the Silver Text is showing us blood and bone are fundamental aspects of growth. Evolution? Transformation?" She looked at her sisters. "What do you think?"

"I think that's intense, extremely deep, and . . . it makes perfect sense." Vanessa picked up a fruit tart and broke a piece off. "We know that we're in Saedo for a reason aside from starting a new life. We were guided here to help activate this Love Spectrum that supposedly will help Celeron, Earth, and all the Cosmos. That's *huge*." She popped the tart into her mouth.

Nina grabbed a pink fruit tart and bit into it. The sweetness made all this serious talk easier to absorb. Was she stress eating? Probably, but the tart was worth it.

"In some stupid and absurd way," Inga pulled the tray of smoked mushroom appetizers closer to her, "I can't help but think the Ulkrins had a hand in helping us. Their abduction led us here."

Sasha crossed her arms. "That's one positive way of looking at it."

Nina washed down the fruit tart with blue water. "I don't know why, but I have this feeling that we're helping Earth in a profound way. We're humans, so if we can help Earth from all the way over here, that's our contribution to humanity."

Nina stayed a while longer to chat with her sisters. Sasha invited her to stay for dinner, which she declined. She had to get back to check on Zeycott. He would have been up already. Nina had stayed a couple of hours longer than she expected, but it was nice catching up with her sisters and getting their perspective on what was happening in Saedo.

As Nina drove Zeycott's rider back to Grandma Ova's house, her DermaPrint ring pulsed with a message from Amelia.

Something's wrong at the hospital. Alarms, noises and shouts. Two doctors are in my room. I don't know them. They're looking around. I'm hiding in a tiny closet with Benjamin. He's sleeping. Don't know what to do.

Ice formed inside Nina's stomach.

Stay where you are. Be right there.

Nina sped up and called Zeycott. He didn't answer.

She called Grandma Ova and learned that Zeycott had woken up earlier than expected. His brothers had called and came to pick him up. The hospital was under attack.

Was Zeycott well enough to battle? Why hadn't he alerted her?

TWENTY-SIX

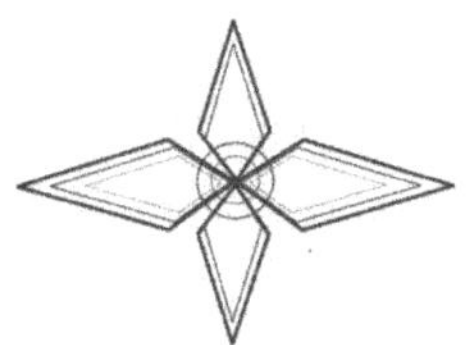

When Nina arrived, she parked the personal rider on the side street. The emergency longships and autobuses crowded the lots in the front and next to the main entrance. She'd never seen so many soldiers in this vicinity.

As she rushed toward the hospital entrance and searched for Zeycott, she saw something from the corner of her eye. A male star-being wearing a gray coat pushed Amelia into the woods, while another male followed behind.

Nina tapped her tattoo ring and sent a message to Zeycott, notifying him of her location and saying that she was running after Amelia. Then she sent a message to Emma and Isabella, hoping they were safe.

Was it really Amelia? Nina wasn't sure, as the distance made it difficult to be certain. But intuition told her it was Amelia. Who were these males?

Nina stumbled on a pipe by the side of a dumpster, grabbed it, and hurried after Amelia. A boom erupted somewhere back at the hospital, and Nina stopped, fearing for Zeycott, Emma, and Isabella's safety. She checked her ring, but no replies appeared from any of them. She pushed her worries aside and continued into the woods using a stone trail.

She came to a manicured outdoor space decked with tables, benches, a shed, and a large gazebo with outdoor exercise equipment. This had to be the outdoor activity area for the hospital patients. Nina spotted Amelia with baby Benjamin inside the gazebo.

The taller star-being pointed to a bench. "Sit."

"What do you want?" Amelia asked, fear coating her words.

The tall star-being turned and Nina recognized him from earlier. She had bumped into him in the main lobby. He ripped off his mask, and his face shifted to Commander Kruegen.

Amelia gasped, jumped off the bench, and moved away from him. The shorter male also shucked off his mask and shifted back to his horrid Ulkrin self, and lunged at Amelia.

"Stop! Leave my baby alone!" Amelia used her body to shield her baby from the evil Ulkrin. Baby Benjamin's cries echoed through the woods.

"He's not yours. He belongs with us, bitch," snarled the Ulkrin with the massive snout.

Nina gripped the pipe with two hands like a bat and ran out to stand beside Amelia. "If you touch her one more time, I'll crack your head open."

Whether that threat was achievable was a different matter. She couldn't let anything happen to Amelia and her baby.

"Let them be, Ferlit." Commander Kruegen pursed his lips as he stared at Amelia's tears, the crying baby in her arm, and Nina. She could only see one eye as his dark hair covered the other.

"But—"

Commander Kruegen sniffed and whipped a dangerous look at his subordinate. "But what?"

"We're here for the offspring. We need to bring him back to Agarrek for more experiments. That was our mission."

"You don't think I know our mission?" Commander Kruegen flared his nostrils, and his eyes blazed with fire as he walked up to Ferlit. "You dare question my authority?"

"N-no, Commander. It's just that you've been acting . . . strange here."

Commander Kruegen let out a disapproving noise.

Nina took the opportunity and rushed Amelia and her baby away.

Snarling, Ferlit leaped in front of them. His claws reached for the baby, but Amelia blocked him and gained a gash to her forearm. Nina whacked Ferlit, hitting his back, but it didn't do a thing except anger him even more.

"Run, Amelia!"

Amelia did, but three more Ulkrins arrived and rushed after her.

Ferlit's eyes flared red as he charged at Nina. Fear and adrenaline coursed through her as she clasped the pipe tight and hit his shoulder. He blocked and grabbed the pipe from her and whipped it aside.

Ferlit came at Nina, grabbed her throat with his claw, and squeezed her. "Bitch."

Nina raked her nails at his face, his arm, and poked his eye as she struggled for breath.

A blast boomed, and Ferlit's body jerked forward.

Another blast erupted, and his head exploded. Blood splattered onto Nina's face and body.

"Are you all right?" Zeycott darted over, his eyes scanning her body while his hands wiped the blood from her face.

Nina nodded urgently. "I'm fine. We have to find Amelia. She ran off with Benjamin. The Ulkrins were chasing her."

Zeycott informed his brothers about more Ulkrins in the woods and instructed them to keep an eye out for Amelia and her baby.

Nina and Zeycott searched the woods together.

"Look!" Nina pointed to the dead Ulkrins on the ground.

Zeycott came up to the dead bodies with their heads blasted off.

Nina glanced around. "Amelia! Where are you?"

"Here." Amelia's hand peeked out from a bush.

Nina and Zeycott rushed over to find her sitting on the ground, huddled between the bushes. Tears streamed down her face as she cradled baby Benjamin.

"Are you okay? Is Benjamin . . . okay?" Nina looked at his quiet state and anxiety constricted her chest.

Amelia looked over at Nina and smiled. "He's fine. He just cried himself out."

"Oh, thank goodness." Nina blew out a sigh of relief.

"Let me help you up." Zeycott assisted Amelia to her feet as he asked, "What happened here?"

"Where's Commander Kruegen?" Nina asked.

"I can't believe I'm saying this, but he let me go . . ." Amelia shrugged. "The three Ulkrins caught up and surrounded me. I couldn't let them take my baby. I was prepared to fight back. But he arrived and just killed them. He killed them without saying anything. Then he came up to me and sniffed at Benjamin. I thought the Ulkrin was going to yank him out of my arms, but he didn't." She sighed, looking exhausted. "I didn't understand it. Initially, he reached out to touch Benjamin, but stopped. He looked confused like he was battling something inside of him. When he did touch my Benjamin, his touch was gentle and . . . interesting."

She paused a moment, looking at her sleeping baby. An odd thought emerged in Nina's mind, but she didn't voice it yet.

Amelia brushed a knuckle down her baby's cheek. "The way he stared at Benjamin made it seem like he'd never seen an infant before. Maybe he hadn't. He'd never visited me or the other girls when I was in that room. Before he left, he looked at me for a long while. It was . . . strange. The dark eyes that had once terrified me were different. For some reason, they didn't frighten me like before. I couldn't explain it other than I didn't sense fear from him. My body didn't shudder, you know?" She blew out a heavy breath. "Maybe fatigue has me rattled. After he left, I gathered myself and sat down on the ground, hoping someone would find me. I expected him to come back for me, but he didn't. Why didn't he?"

Nina looked up at Zeycott, whose expression showed something percolating in his mind.

"You said he sniffed Benjamin?" Zeycott asked.

"Yes. He even brushed his knuckles down Benjamin's face and around the textured skin there. When Benjamin babbled something in his sleep, Commander Kruegen sucked in a breath, retracted his claw, and stepped away. Something sparked in his eyes, but then darkness returned. Oh, he has a birthmark on his forehead too. I noticed it when he pushed his hair aside. I'd never seen his full face up until that moment. His hair had always covered it."

Nina tossed out a wild theory. "Could Benjamin be his offspring? His son?"

Amelia stared at her baby.

"Ulkrins can scent their offspring," Zeycott said.

Nina looked at the baby. "Baby Benjamin has the same birthmark as Commander Kruegen."

Emotions washed over Amelia's face, ranging from disbelief to confusion to worry. "I didn't know whose sperm was implanted in me. They used a device that violated me and the other girls. Some were raped, but I don't remember that happening to me. I would have . . . I think. I was in and out of consciousness most of the time. I overheard them saying the device would deliver faster results."

She could only imagine what Amelia had gone through. Nina and her sisters could have been in that exact situation. Would they have survived?

Nina offered Amelia comfort and truth. "It doesn't matter who the father is. *You're* his mother. You gave birth to him. He's going to receive love and grow up to be a decent star-being."

A smile ghosted on Amelia's lips. "Thank you. I'll do my best, but I'm scared. Will he be back for his son? And if he does come back, would he bring an army?"

Zeycott placed a hand on Amelia's shoulders. "If he wanted to take the baby away, he would have done so already. It would have been easy to do it while no one else was here. He wouldn't waste time and energy to bring in an army.

Maybe seeing his offspring shifted something in his mind. Maybe he didn't want to bring Benjamin back to Agarrek."

"Yeah. The other Ulkrin said something about more experiments. Maybe he didn't want his son to experience that. Maybe . . . maybe he has a heart."

Nina shuddered at that statement. These were the same species who had abducted her and her siblings. She knew the Ulkrins and their beasts for their viciousness, but something was developing on planet Celeron.

The Love Spectrum flashed in her mind. Could the activation of this cosmic force bring awareness to a species that had always embraced evil? Was that possible?

Baby Benjamin opened his eyes and cried.

"He's hungry." Amelia dropped a kiss to his cheek. "Let's get you fed."

After they made sure Amelia was situated safely in her room again, Zeycott took Nina home.

TWENTY-SEVEN

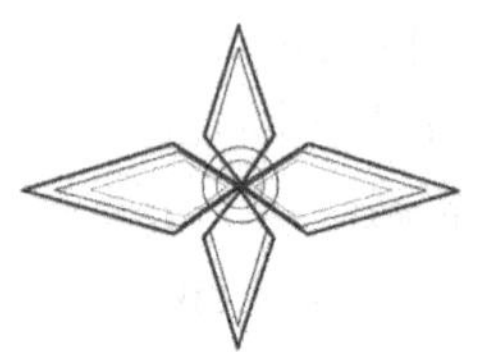

After a quick shower, Nina sat down and took out the portable x-ray scanner. "I need to check on you."

"You don't have to. I'm fine. The White Mutaat spider is a game-changer. I'm cured, Nina. But I still have something that will forever engulf me . . ."

His serious expression twisted her stomach. "What? What's wrong now?"

"I'll never be cured of you, love." He beamed a wide smile.

She smacked his chest playfully. "You scared me. After what happened today, my heart can't take any more shocking news."

Zeycott pulled her in for an embrace. "You'll always be a part of me, Nina. You're my corra."

"And you're mine. You can't get rid of me. Ever." She held up the device. "Still, I'm checking your bones. I need to see them."

He sighed and surrendered to her. After seeing how his bones were free of the disease, Nina jumped, jiggled around her living room, and hopped onto his lap. She showered him with kisses on his face. "I'm so happy."

"Me too." His smile stretched from ear to ear. "I could live the rest of my life with you kissing me like this."

"Then that's what we'll do." Nina wrapped her arms around his neck and noticed a scab and rubbed it with her finger. "What happened here?"

"A cut from flying debris when a monitoring machine got hit by blaster and exploded in the hospital."

"Was anyone hurt?" She recalled the loud explosion during her chase after Amelia.

"Just minor injuries. We had a lot of undercover soldiers placed around the hospital. We didn't know what the Ulkrins had planned, but we had a hunch that they'd want the baby. The undercover soldiers caught the Ulkrins disguised as doctors and nurses. A few of them can shape-shift too." He ran his hand down her back. "We didn't expect them to bring an army of Ulkrins in disguise."

"I think Commander Kruegen will be back. Or he'll send someone to check on his son. What do you think?"

"I don't think he knew Benjamin was his son until he got a whiff of the familial scent. He probably came here to retrieve the baby, but when he discovered it was his, something changed in him. Whatever it was, we have to be grateful for it. Maybe it was a momentary slip. Maybe he needed time to reevaluate his plan. Or maybe he had to go back and report his discovery before making another decision. There are many possibilities." Zeycott sighed. "They lost a large faction of their army today. They'll need to recuperate. In the meantime, my brothers and I are planning something too."

Nina wanted to know, but not today. She was tired, and her brain didn't have room for any more Ulkrin news.

She studied Zeycott's beautiful features, and she couldn't help but wonder if they'd make an adorable baby like Benjamin. She wasn't ready to have a baby now, but it was a thought she'd consider for the future.

Zeycott's eyes warmed, and he smiled. "I think we'd make beautiful babies."

Her cheeks flushed with heat. "How did you know?"

"I can see it in your eyes. I'm learning to recognize your thoughts. The way you're studying me, taking in the details as though you're imagining what features our future child would have. Would he have my eyes, your nose, my skin color —all those things." He ran a thumb over her bottom lip. "When the time comes, would you like to have a baby with me?"

Nina's heart swelled as she looked into his sage eyes that had darkened significantly. "I'd love to." She used to believe that marriage had to happen first before she brought a baby into this world. But living in Saedo had opened her to many things. Though she didn't mind getting hitched with Zeycott, it wasn't a requirement anymore. As long as they continued loving each other, she was happy.

"I can't wait for you to move in with me," he said, his eyes gleaming with hope.

She narrowed her eyes and poked a finger at his chest. "Is that a question or a statement?"

He smirked. "It started out as a question in my head, but then the image was too perfect and too real. I couldn't see it as anything else. Don't squash my dream, please."

Joy ignited in her stomach, filling every part of her body

with hope and love. "I'll make your dreams come true because you've made mine."

"I'm renovating my house. There's a new addition with a large studio and *very* high ceilings." His eyebrows wiggled. "For our own private version of flying yoga. That'll be your place to create and explore. You can do whatever you want there."

She gripped his face and crushed a sloppy kiss to his lips. "I'll have to come up with an extensive plan to use the space well. Thank you. I got a notification that my yoga channel reached over three million subscribers! I'm making tons of credits from the sales of my classes too. More than what I'd make at Compact Fitness Center. I'm going to resign from my position and focus on my yoga videos."

"That means I get to have lunch with you when I'm working at home."

"Yes. And if you behave, you might end up getting some afternoon 'dessert.'" She grinned.

"Oh . . . then I need to make sure I work from home more often."

His smile and his presence filled her heart and soul. There was nowhere else she'd rather be than right here on this planet with her man. With him, she'd found her heart, her home, and her stability. She found a starmate who not only valued her sense of exploration, but he enjoyed being part of it as well.

I deserve a man who loves me and supports my sense of exploration. Thank you, Universe, for hearing my prayer and giving me my heart and soul.

She rested her forehead on his. "Have you seen our field of blessiums?"

His eyes widened. "No. We have a field of them? Where?"

She hopped down from his lap. "Wanna go see them now?"

He glanced out the window that showed the night had settled in.

"We can still see them. They're by the pink grass field, so there's going to be light."

Nina and Zeycott stopped by to say hello to Grandma Ova before heading over to the field of blessiums. She brought along four pots and two small shovels.

"We can grow some indoors and some outdoors when you finish renovating. I want a field of them in the backyard. Maybe we can add some to the front lawn for a nice curb appeal."

Zeycott smiled. "Whatever you want, my yoga queen. My home is your home. This is the beginning of the rest of our lives, right? You can't get rid of me. I'm etched in your bones, and you're etched in mine."

"We're bonded for life," she said as she inhaled the lovely aroma of the blessiums before she even saw them.

He sniffed. "That's some scent. It's sweet, charming, intelligent, handsome—"

Laughing, she elbowed him. "Stop describing yourself."

He smirked, knowing exactly what he was saying. "I'm describing us. Our love gave birth to these gorgeous flowers, so they represent us in every aspect." He came up to the bunch that grew beside the pink grass. He turned on the light from his wristband and cast a brighter glow on the area. "There are so many of them."

"Yup. Let's dig up these blessings that were bestowed upon us."

"It's not what I imagined doing at nine in the evening." He crouched, stabbed the shovel into the dirt, and pulled out two flowers with roots and all. "But with you, it's perfect."

After they filled the pots with enough blessiums, the area glowed even brighter. Nina glanced up at the sky, tugged at Zeycott's arm, and gasped. "Oh, wow! Look, Zeycott."

"Amazing."

A massive ribbon of energy hung in the sky, several layers of colors glowing within it.

"It's so beautiful. It's like the Aurora Borealis, but a hundred times brighter. And it looks like it's dancing. Does this happen often in Saedo? I've never seen it before."

Zeycott wrapped an arm around her shoulders. "I've never seen it either."

The ribbon of energy expanded, creating several images within it.

"Do you see the faces?" Nina's heart pounded at the realization. "I know what it is now."

"The Love Spectrum," he said.

A melody rang in her ears, but she wasn't sure if she was imagining it. "Do you hear the music?"

He nodded. "It's very soft."

"It's like we have to pay attention to hear it. Once we do, we can't stop listening." The music soothed her body the way the aroma of the pink grass did.

"A cosmic song from the Love Spectrum," Zeycott said. "I

wonder what magic will bless Saedo when it's fully activated."

Though Nina knew danger still lurked, peace and comfort blanketed her, knowing that something this magical was overhead, watching over her, her loved ones, and all of Saedo. No matter what came next, she'd be victorious. With Zeycott by her side, there was nothing she couldn't achieve, nothing she couldn't endure.

Their love had activated the middle layer of the spectrum, which displayed a kaleidoscope of colors and textures. The night sky had transformed for them, and she wanted to soak in the magic as much as she could.

A stream of silver symbols flowed across the sky. She knew in her heart that they were part of the Silver Text, which meant the ancestors of the land were a part of the Love Spectrum.

"Do you want to spend another night sleeping out here? We can go back to Grandma Ova's and borrow some blankets."

"That sounds like a splendid idea. If you encounter another portal, don't run off without me."

"I'm not going anywhere without you, my yoga king." They headed back to Grandma Ova's house.

Zeycott leaned in. "Do you want to try some yoga moves out here?"

"Maybe another time. I don't want the Love Spectrum or the ancestors to think that we're disrespecting them."

"I'm borrowing a big tent from Grandma Ova then. They can't see anything if we're inside the tent."

Nina laughed at his persistence. "How about we just get our supplies and go from there?"

A little while later, as she settled into the tent, which had a huge zip-out section at the top for them to stargaze, she thanked the Cosmos for Zeycott. The night turned out to be an explorative evening where Zeycott got to have the yogasmic experience he'd wanted.

Thank you so much for reading Nina and Zeycott's story! I can't wait to share Isabella and Tammo's romance with you in **An Alien Future**. Sign up for my **newsletter** to receive release dates, giveaways & more!

http://callazae.com/newsletter/

Blurb

His heart is engulfed with the dark… but for her, it awakens with light.

Disheartened with relationships, Cathy Lu concentrates on her career. But the magic around the August Full Moon lures her to a stunning angel who illuminates her desires in a way that makes her wonder if everything is just an illusion.

As a seraph bound to blood, death, and responsibility, Daedriel has never had a long-term lover. But one kiss from Cathy unlocks everything for him, making him want the forever.

Can he keep her safe while evil swarms around them? Or should he keep her away from him, away from all the darkness that threatens him?

Excerpt

Cathy

Cathy Lu hammered a nail into the plank of wood on her back deck and thought about her ex-boyfriend—specifically his family jewels. How would he feel if she pounded him like this nail? Yes, it was a morbid thought, but as an ex-girlfriend who had been betrayed, she had every right to feel that way. Cheaters deserved a painful punishment, didn't they? They had to feel all the pain they'd bestowed on their significant other. That should be a law. So, she envisioned all the things that made her feel better. Wasn't that part of the healing process?

She pounded another nail into the wood and admired her work. She'd learned a few handy things during her two-year relationship with Gavin. He had promised to renovate her deck and the new studio she was adding to her house. But promises from a cheating man rusted over time. It made her wary of men's promises in general. Now, she depended on herself.

Cathy had kicked Gavin out of her home four months ago when she discovered several text messages and emails he'd been sending to two other women. She should have suspected something was up when he came home later than usual or when he had unexpected phone calls that took him into another room. She had been too trusting.

She considered herself an intelligent woman, but when she discovered the truth about Gavin, it made her feel stupid. Love had a way of distorting things, and she couldn't afford another loss like that. She was careful now. She had to be. Her heart had shattered, and she had hammered it back together. She sighed at the symbolism of hurting Gavin and also piecing herself together by hammering a single nail. Maybe that idea could make its way into her new greeting card collection.

Despite it all, she had moved on, mending herself one step at a time. Time spent alone gave her the retrospection and the clarity to focus on her company, Luminous Press. She had a small team of people who worked for her, making sure her journals, novelty books, greeting cards, and other miscellaneous products were delivered on time to their vendors. She and her mother, Celia, had started the company eight years ago, when she was twenty-five years old. Working with her mom had taught her how to be a successful businesswoman and a decent person who looked at things with compassion.

Be gentle to everyone. You never know what someone is going through. You can't measure someone else's pain from a personal scale.

Everything was different when it was personal, wasn't it? The measuring scale changed when you were the one experiencing the pain. It was all perspective. No one could ever understand that misery until they'd experienced it themselves. Standing on the outside made it difficult to see the storm from within.

Her mother's wise words echoed in her mind. If only her mom were still alive, she'd comfort Cathy, reminding her that not all men were the same.

Victor Perez knocked on the glass panel of her sliding door, opened it, and stepped out to the deck. "I'm all done for the day, Cathy. The two bathrooms, kitchen, and living room are all spotless now." He smiled and removed the apron, folding it into his hand.

Cathy rose to her feet and stretched her back. She appreciated his gesture even though she knew that his wife, Rosa, needed him more. Rosa and Victor had been cleaning Cathy's house for the last two years until she fell sick with a thyroid disorder that had gotten worse in the last few months. They had planned on early retirement, but life threw a curveball at them that readjusted their plans. So now, it was just Victor supporting his family. Their daughter, Lizzi, who was also Cathy's friend, lived in New York. She'd come home to visit and assist them whenever she could.

"Do you need me to help you with anything else before I head home?" Victor asked.

The weight of his wife's illness sagged on his face even with that adorable smile. The eyes and facial features revealed a lot of things that people didn't realize.

Cathy tapped the hammer against her hand. "I've got it handled. Thank you, though. Please send my best to Rosa. How's she doing?"

Victor sighed, and his shoulders drooped. "She's improving slowly. Her hair isn't falling out as much now with the new medication. We have a doctor's appointment next Friday to follow up. I'm praying for good news."

Cathy squeezed his arm. "Please keep me posted. Rosa's a strong woman. I'm sure she'll overcome this."

He nodded, giving her a warm smile. "Thank you."

"You don't have to come next week. I'll see you in two weeks," Cathy said and noticed the worry lines on his forehead. "Don't worry. The payment won't change. I figure you could use that time to be with Rosa. Besides, I live here alone. How much of a mess can I possibly make in a week?" She knew most people hired a cleaning service every two weeks, but she kept Victor and Rosa on once a week. She liked them and didn't mind supporting their business. They had been cleaning for her mom before Cathy hired them for her own house.

His eyes watered. "I don't know what to say."

"Say that you'll make the best of it. Life is short, Victor. Be with your family when you can."

After Victor left, Cathy resumed her work. She tried to take the same advice she gave to others, which was why she planned a three-week vacation to regroup. She hadn't taken a break in a long time, so this vacation was a treat. Her best friend, Sydney, the vice president of Luminous Press, could manage while Cathy was away.

Cathy planned on using this extra time to brainstorm the greeting card collections for the next few seasons. Designing the art for the greeting cards was one of the fun parts of her business. It activated a different area in her brain that wasn't crammed with numbers, profit margins, production, deliveries, and so on.

A bird squawked somewhere, and the unique sound broke through the silence. She rose from the deck and glanced toward the woods that drew her to this place. Beyond the trees was the gorgeous Prudent Lake. She had brought a tent out there a few times and slept under the moon and stars. She was due for another adventure soon, especially with the August Moon Festival next week.

When she was six years old, she looked out her bedroom window at the full moon and saw a gold rim around it. It glowed for a while, mesmerizing her. At that time, she had felt a warmth brush against her face when the rim glowed, but it could've been the imagination of a child believing in magic and fairytales. Because of that childhood experience, Cathy felt an odd friendship with it. The moon pulled at her in an inexplicable way.

With nature as her background, Cathy found the stability to move on after her mother's death a year ago. They used to come to Prudent Lake on vacation when she was little, so living here was somehow reliving the precious moments they'd shared together. She had no idea where her father had gone. He left when she was six, and that broke her mother.

Another squawk rang out, and she looked around, trying to see the bird or hawk that was making the lovely sound. She spotted nothing. She went into her kitchen, took out the bag of birdseed, and filled her bird feeder. "Enjoy your snacks."

She loved watching the birds gathered in her backyard like it was their playground. The enchanting sounds of nature were the spa that relaxed her.

Her phone rang, and Sydney's name flashed on the screen. "Hey, I don't mean to interrupt your vacation, but I just wanted to remind you about the August Moon Festival next Friday in Boston. Are you going?"

The August Moon Festival was a special time of the year for her family and her heritage. In the past, she'd attend the event with her mother. But this year, Cathy wanted to do something personal, something without the crowd. She could celebrate the holiday right in her backyard.

"I'm going to pass. I'll just do something small at home."

"Are you sure?" Disappointment leaked from Sydney's voice. They had met in college and became fast friends.

Cathy appreciated Sydney's intelligence and foresight when it came to business. Outside of business, Sydney was the trusted friend every woman deserved. Without Sydney's support in both business and friendship, Cathy didn't know if Luminous Press would be as successful as it was.

"Yes, I'm not in the mood for crowds this year."

"Hang out with us girls," Sydney said. "We love talking shit about cheaters, and there's *a lot* of them. That means we'll have plenty of conversations and drinks."

Cathy laughed, appreciating her friend. "We'll hang out soon, I promise. I need to hire a contractor to finish my studio. I want to get it done before I return to work. And I'm brainstorming the new greeting card collection too."

"You're *supposed* to be on vacation," Sydney said with a disapproving tone.

"Yes, *Mom*. I know, I know. I don't mind it, though. The creative part is fun for me. You know that."

"I do, and that's why I'm not driving over there and dragging you away. Do you want me to bring you back any mooncakes, lanterns, food, or anything?"

"No, thanks. I already placed an order for the mooncakes. They're being shipped to me. Have fun, and don't forget to make your wish to the Moon Goddess. You never know. She could make your dreams come true."

"I'll be sure to make a long list for her. She should find something on there to give me," Sydney said.

"You are the queen of lists." Cathy could imagine the several pages of demands from Sydney.

Read now! **Unlock the Angel**
www.callazae.com/books

ACKNOWLEDGMENTS

Thank you to Anna, Lindsay, Jenny, and Sharon who helped my story shine. You are the shiny siSTARS in my galaxy. Thank you to my family who always give me everything I need to pursue my dreams. You are my entire Universe.

And thank you, dear readers, you give me a reason to keep writing. Without you, there's no one to appreciate the stardust within my creation. You have my utmost gratitude. Thank you, thank you, thank you.

ABOUT THE AUTHOR
CALLA ZAE

Calla Zae writes otherworldly romance. She loves delving into fantastical worlds where her imagination roams wild. Calla is also an artist who enjoys playing with colors, textures, and patterns. She has a love for mysticism, astrology, astronomy, Kdrama, Cdramas, true crime TV shows, romantic suspense novels, cats, and nature.

Calla lives in Massachusetts with her husband who keeps her grounded to Earth and two creative children who think she has her own secret planet. They're onto something...